FRIEN OF ACPL

T5-BCF-583

Millie's Reluctant Sacrifice

Millie's Reluctant Sacrifice

BOOK SEVEN
of the
*A Life of Faith:
Millie Keith*
Series

Based on the characters by
Martha Finley

Mission City Press
Franklin, Tennessee

Book Seven of the *A Life of Faith: Millie Keith* Series

Millie's Reluctant Sacrifice
Copyright © 2003, Mission City Press, Inc. All Rights Reserved.

Published by Mission City Press, Inc.

No part of this publication may be reproduced, stored in a retrieval system, or transmitted in any form or by any means — electronic, mechanical, photocopying, recording, or any other — without the prior written permission of the publisher.

This book is based on the *Mildred Keith* novels written by Martha Finley and first published in 1876 by Dodd, Mead & Company.

Adaptation Written by: Kersten Hamilton
Cover & Interior Design: Richmond & Williams
Cover Photography: Michelle Grisco Photography
Typesetting: BookSetters

Unless otherwise indicated, all Scripture references are from the Holy Bible, New International Version (NIV). Copyright © 1973, 1978, 1984 by International Bible Society. Used by permission of Zondervan Publishing House, Grand Rapids, MI. All rights reserved.

Millie Keith and *A Life of Faith* are trademarks of Mission City Press, Inc.

For more information, write to Mission City Press at P.O. Box 681913, Franklin, Tennessee 37068-1913, or visit our Web Site at:

www.alifeoffaith.com

Library of Congress Catalog Card Number: 2003107250
Finley, Martha
     Millie's Reluctant Sacrifice
     Book Seven of the *A Life of Faith: Millie Keith* Series
     ISBN: 1-928749-15-1

Printed in the United States of America
1 2 3 4 5 6 7 8 — 07 06 05 04 03

DEDICATION

This book is
dedicated to
the memory of
MARTHA FINLEY
1828—1909

*Martha Finley was a woman of God
clearly committed to advancing the cause of Christ
through stories of people who sought
to reflect Christian character in everyday life.
Although written in an era very different from ours,
her works still inspire both young and old
to seek to know and follow the living God.*

— FOREWORD —

*W*elcome to *Millie's Reluctant Sacrifice*, the seventh book in *A Life of Faith: Millie Keith* Series. You are invited to join Millie as she becomes the wife of Dr. Charles Landreth and sets out on a new adventure with him. Our story resumes in the summer of 1843, in Pleasant Plains, Indiana, as Millie prepares for her wedding. Millie has spent years anticipating what she believes will be a life of singleness with Jesus. Now she finds that God's plans are far more exciting than even she had imagined!

∞ BOLIVIA: HISTORICAL BACKGROUND ∞

Bolivia is nestled on the western side of South America. In order to reach Bolivia in Millie's day, it was necessary for her to travel by ship from New York down to Cape Horn on the tip of South America and back north in the Pacific Ocean to the port of Arica in Chile. Then an overland trip was required across a narrow stretch of Chile and through the mountains to La Paz and beyond.

Although two-thirds of Bolivia is tropical or semi-tropical, most of the population has always lived on the *altiplano*, or high plateau, a vast tableland with an average altitude of 13,000 feet. The *altiplano* is protected from the outside world by high mountain ranges of the Andes that run along Bolivia's border with Chile and Peru.

There are treasures in Bolivia. It was in the relatively fertile ground around Lake Titicaca that the potato, which would later feed much of Europe, was first cultivated; and the mountains were laced with riches of silver. But the most wonderful treasure by far is the people themselves.

Foreword

Great civilizations have risen here, and crumbled into dust.

In A.D. 100 the Tiahuanaco culture spread southward from the shores of the lake, unifying the region for the first time. The Tiahuanaco culture collapsed after A.D. 1200.

Over the next three centuries, the area was host to many different regional states, empires, and belief systems. It was not completely united again until the late 1460s when the powerful, warlike Incas rose to power.

In the one hundred years that they ruled, the Incas performed some of the most amazing engineering and agricultural projects the Americas had ever seen. They built systems of roads, cleared and cultivated thousands of acres of new agricultural lands, built cities, erected vast storehouses for food, and created complex calendars to chart the seasons.

But as advanced as their science and engineering skills were, the Incas also bowed to an incredible evil. Like the ancient Egyptians, they believed that their king was a god, and they worshiped a vast array of demonic entities. The most powerful Inca cult worshiped Inti, the sun god. Another cult was devoted to Pachamama, who they considered mother of the earth. They also worshiped the dead, their ancestors, and nature, including the harsh gods of the mountains.

The ultimate sacrifice the Incas could make to please these mountain gods was to offer up their own children as sacrifices. The children were carried as high in the mountains as humans could climb, and there they were given drugs and left to die. Even today, their mummified remains are a silent testimony to the horrible spiritual darkness that once gripped this land.

Millie's Reluctant Sacrifice

The Inca rule was brought to an end by the Spanish conquest of the 1530s, but the Good News of Jesus has still not been proclaimed to all the people of Bolivia. Pray for the people of Bolivia, and the missionaries who are living and working there today.

∾ WOMEN IN MISSIONS ∾

Millie's ambition to be a single female missionary to China was quite forward-thinking in the 1840s. China was the largest Protestant mission field in the world between 1830 and 1949, but single female missionaries were practically unheard of. In fact, the very concept of foreign missions was only a few decades old at the time of Millie's story.

In the year 1801, there were no missionaries from the United States serving on any foreign field. Around 1811, a young seminary student named Adoniram Judson wrote: "How do Christians discharge this trust committed to them? They let three-fourths of the world sleep the sleep of death, ignorant of the simple truth that a Savior died for them. Content if they can be useful in the little circle of their acquaintances, they quietly sit and see whole nations perish for lack of knowledge."

Judson met and married a young woman named Ann Hasseltine, who was called to foreign missions as well. They both understood the danger they would face. When Adoniram asked Ann's parents for her hand in marriage, he wrote: "I have naught but to ask, whether you can consent to part with your daughter early next spring, to see her no more in this world; whether you can consent to her departure, and her subjection to the hardships and sufferings of

missionary life; whether you can consent to her exposure to the dangers of the ocean; to the fatal influence of the climate of India; to every kind of want and distress; to degradation, insult, persecution, and perhaps a violent death. Can you consent to all this, for the sake of Him who left His heavenly home and died for her and for you; for the sake of perishing immortal souls, for the sake of Zion, and the glory of God?"

Thirteen days after they wed in 1812, when Ann and Adoniram set sail for India, she became the first female foreign missionary from the United States. Ann was a full partner to her husband in the missionary work. She became the first missionary to learn Siamese, translating the book of Matthew into that language. She fought tirelessly to improve the lives of Burmese women, who were treated little better than animals. Ann Judson died on the mission field October 24, 1826. She had broken ground as a missionary from the United States, but much was still to be done.

Married women frequently accompanied their husbands to the mission field, but single women were simply not accepted by the newly forming mission societies. By the 1860s, however, so many young women were offering their lives as missions workers that the Women's Missionary Movement was formed, and began to create "female agencies," mission societies that sponsored only single women. Nevertheless, society as a whole still did not approve.

It was considered scandalous in 1878 when Hudson Taylor allowed single female missionaries to work in teams in the interior of China. Nonetheless, in only four years the China Inland Mission had 95 single women on their ministry lists, much to the disapproval of some other mission-

aries. "Hudson Taylor makes extraordinarily ample use of the services of unmarried ladies," a German missionary wrote in 1898. He felt the idea of single women working in the mission field "unbecoming and repellent." It was not repellent to God, however, and He continued to call women into His service. By 1900, women outnumbered men in the foreign mission field by two to one.

The words of Hallie Winsborough, First Secretary of Woman's Work in the Presbyterian Church in the United States, are very true. "No fiction was ever half so incredible," Ms. Winsborough said, "as the story of what God can do with plain, ordinary women when they let Him have His way in their lives." Here are some of these ordinary women, who lived heroic lives of courage and faith. You may want to find books about each of them!

Clara Swain left the United States in 1869 as the world's first female missionary doctor. She traveled to India, where male doctors were not allowed to treat women. In the first year, she treated 1,300 patients and trained seventeen medical students. In just five years, she built the Women's Hospital and Medical School, the first in all of Asia.

Charlotte Diggs "Lottie" Moon left her job, home, and parents in 1873 to tell the Chinese about Jesus. At first the local people feared her, calling her "devil woman," but she was determined to remain in China as long as it took—until all the people knew of Jesus. She adopted traditional Chinese dress, learned their language and customs, and won many hearts for Jesus.

Amy Carmichael was commissioned by the Church of England Missionary Society in 1895 to go to Dohnavur, India, where she served fifty-six years without a furlough. After Amy had ministered in India for some time, she

learned of a terrible practice at the pagan temples in India. Young girls were taken and made temple prostitutes, where they led horrible lives of slavery. Amy became God's kidnapper, stealing the girls and hiding them in places where they could be raised in safety. Many western Christians turned their backs on her work because they could not believe the stories she told.

Ruth Pettigrew, commissioned as a missionary to China in 1920, was fearless in her mission to preach God's Word. Ruth traveled alone through China, staying in homes, chapels, and country inns. Neither robbers nor kidnappers could stop her from carrying the Gospel to Chinese women and children.

∞ MISSIONS ON THE HOME FRONT IN MILLIE'S DAY ∞

In 1843, religious freedom was enjoyed in more countries than ever before. The Bible had been printed in many languages, and missionaries were traveling from the British Isles and the United States all over the world, intent on obeying the Great Commission of Matthew 28:18-20.

But a strange thing was happening in the very countries that sent out the missionaries. The great-grandchildren of those who had fought for religious freedom were growing sleepy and complacent in their faith, unwilling to take a stand for Jesus in their own hometowns.

In Millie Keith's day, if a girl was determined to live a pure, godly life, she would often have had to take a stand against fashions, sinful behavior at parties, and even what society considered to be in good taste!

Society was willing to bow politely to the church, so long as Christians did nothing to convict or confront people with

their sins. Christians became conditioned by society to live in such a way as to offend no one—and to convert no one. If they were to fit into society, their lights had to be hidden under a bushel.

In 1825, evangelist Charles G. Finney wrote an article intended to wake up Christians to the many ways they were compromising their faith. He pretended to write advice "not to convert anybody," but he meant his 67 rules to convict his readers and help them become better Christians, as they realized what they should *not* do. By reading some of his suggestions from "How to Preach so as to Convert Nobody," we can understand what a Christian girl in 1843 might have faced as she tried to live for the Lord. Do you think it is similar to what you face today?

Rule 1. Let your supreme motive be to secure your own popularity; then, of course, your preaching will be adapted to that end, and not to convert souls to Christ.

Rule 2. Aim at pleasing, rather than at converting, your hearers.

Rule 9. Make no distinct points, and take no disturbing issues with the consciences of your hearers, lest they remember these issues and become alarmed about their souls.

Rule 12. Avoid preaching doctrines that are offensive to the carnal mind, lest they should say of you, as they did of Christ, "This is a hard saying. Who can hear it?" and that you are injuring your influence.

Rule 19. Aim to make your hearers pleased with themselves and pleased with you, and be careful not to wound the feelings of any one.

Rule 22. Do not make the impression that God commands your hearers now and here to obey the truth.

Rule 23. Do not make the impression that you expect your hearers to commit themselves upon the spot and give their hearts to God.

Rule 28. Make the impression that, if God is as good as you are, He will send no one to Hell.

Rule 32. Try to convert sinners to Christ without producing any uncomfortable convictions of sin.

Rule 62. Be tame and timid in presenting the claims of God, as would become you in presenting your own claims.

Rule 63. Be careful not to testify from your own personal experience of the power of the Gospel, lest you should produce the conviction upon your hearers that you have something which they need.

∽ MISSIONS TODAY ∽

Unfortunately, we do not have to imagine very much to see what happens when the Christians in a culture bow to the world and live "as to convert nobody." Today, missionaries from all over the world are sent to the United States to tell people about Jesus! Christians were never meant to blend quietly into the culture around them, whether that culture is one saturated with witchcraft in the mountains of Bolivia or materialism on the streets of the United States. People are dying around us, and we must live the truth if they are to be set free. Your life—the witness you live before your friends today—may mean the difference between life and death for your friends.

KEITH FAMILY TREE

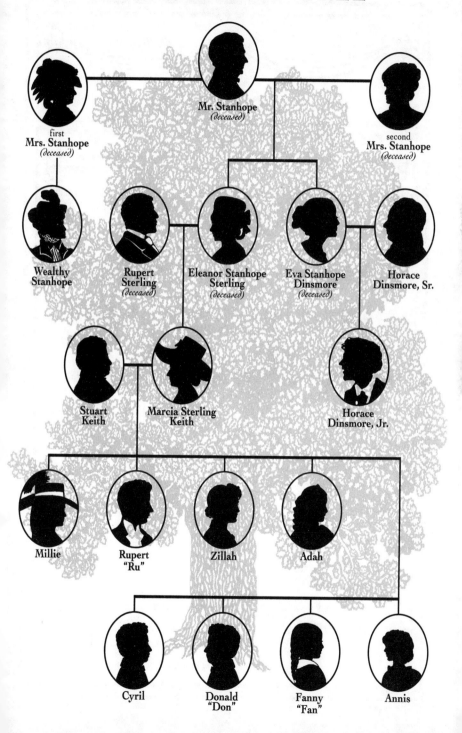

first
Mr. Stanhope
(deceased)

Mr. Stanhope
(deceased)

second
Mrs. Stanhope
(deceased)

**Wealthy
Stanhope**

**Rupert
Sterling**
(deceased)

**Eleanor Stanhope
Sterling**
(deceased)

**Eva Stanhope
Dinsmore**
(deceased)

**Horace
Dinsmore, Sr.**

**Stuart
Keith**

**Marcia Sterling
Keith**

**Horace
Dinsmore, Jr.**

Millie

**Rupert
"Ru"**

Zillah

Adah

Cyril

**Donald
"Don"**

**Fanny
"Fan"**

Annis

SETTING

*O*ur story begins in early summer of 1843 in Pleasant Plains, Indiana, the hometown of Millie Keith and her family.

CHARACTERS

∞ THE KEITH FAMILY ∞

Stuart Keith—the father of the Keith family and a respected attorney-at-law.

Marcia Keith—the mother of the Keith family and the step-niece of Aunt Wealthy Stanhope.

The Keith children:

> **Mildred Eleanor ("Millie")**—age 22
> **Rupert ("Ru")**—age 21
> **Zillah**—age 19; married to Wallace Ormsby
> **Adah**—age 18
> **Cyril** and **Donald ("Don")**—age 17, twin boys
> **Fanny ("Fan")**—age 15
> **Annis**—age 11

∞ PLEASANT PLAINS, INDIANA ∞

Charles Landreth—age 27; a friend of the Keith family.

Reverend Matthew and Celestia Ann Lord—a local minister and his wife.

> **Joy Everlasting**—their 6-year-old daughter

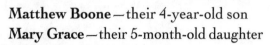

Matthew Boone — their 4-year-old son

Mary Grace — their 5-month-old daughter

Nicholas Ransquate and his wife **Damaris Drybread Ransquate** — friends of the Keiths.

Runhilda — their 6-year-old daughter

Otis Lochneer — Charles Landreth's boyhood friend.

Gordon Lightcap and his wife **Gavriel Mikolaus Lightcap.**

Jedidiah ("Jed") Mikolaus — age 15, brother of Gavriel

Jasmine ("Jaz") Mikolaus — age 11, sister of Gavriel

Rhoda Jane Lightcap — age 24; Millie's best friend in Pleasant Plains; she runs the local stagecoach way station along with her brother.

Emmaretta Lightcap — age 18

Minerva ("Min") Lightcap — age 16

York Monocker and his wife **Claudina Chetwood Monocker.**

Will Chetwood and his wife **Lucilla Grange Chetwood.**

Joseph Grange and his wife **Helen Monocker Grange.**

Wallace Ormsby and his wife **Zillah Keith Ormsby.**

Dr. and Mrs. Chetwood — the town physician and his wife.

Mrs. Prior — the landlady of the Union Hotel.

Frank Osborne — a Keith family friend from Ohio.

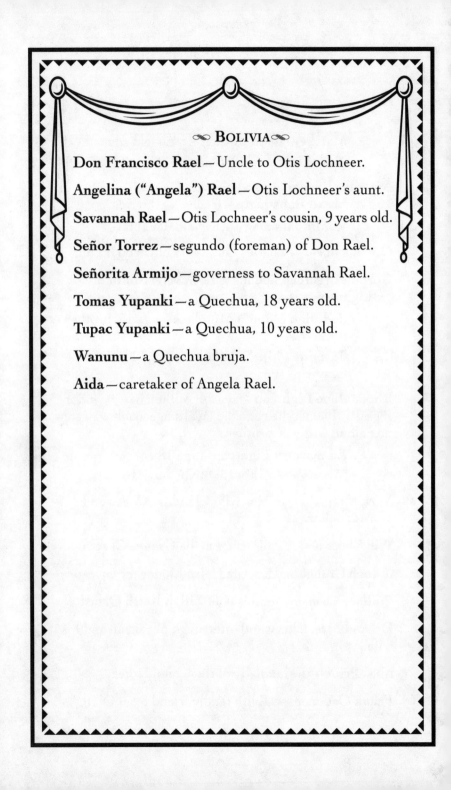

∞ BOLIVIA∞

Don Francisco Rael — Uncle to Otis Lochneer.

Angelina ("Angela") Rael — Otis Lochneer's aunt.

Savannah Rael — Otis Lochneer's cousin, 9 years old.

Señor Torrez — segundo (foreman) of Don Rael.

Señorita Armijo — governess to Savannah Rael.

Tomas Yupanki — a Quechua, 18 years old.

Tupac Yupanki — a Quechua, 10 years old.

Wanunu — a Quechua bruja.

Aida — caretaker of Angela Rael.

CHAPTER

1

Uncertainties

Do not those who plot evil go
astray? But those who plan
what is good find love
and faithfulness.

PROVERBS 14:22

Uncertainties

*M*illie Keith leaned back on the green grass and closed her eyes. *You pay such attention to detail, Lord. If You had forgotten one little thing, I suspect creation would collapse into nothingness. But You didn't.* The warmth of the afternoon sun had drawn out scents of the leaves—blackberry, sage, and wild mint—and mixed them with the breeze, a fresh breath that came over the marsh bringing the northern wildness with it. *You truly have a time for everything.*

"Tragedy!"

Millie opened her eyes. Jasmine Mikolaus was studying her as if she were the guest of honor at a wake. The eleven-year-old's brow was wrinkled. Millie's own younger sisters, Fan and Annis, stood beside her. They had taken a break from their berry-picking to gather flowers.

"Millie's not dying," Annis said. "She's just getting married."

"Which is practically the same thing!" Jaz collapsed onto the soft grass beside Millie, flowers spilling out of her apron.

"How is marriage a tragedy?" Millie picked up two flowers and started twining the stems to make a garland. "Most people consider it a joyful occasion."

Jaz, her eyes dark and solemn, put her chin on her knees and studied Millie. "Do you remember the bear?"

"Of course, I do." Millie could not help glancing, just to be sure there were no horrible beady eyes peering out at them from the underbrush. The bear had attacked them in the marsh on a day very much like today. "But I don't understand your point."

Millie's Reluctant Sacrifice

"My point is," Jasmine said, "married ladies never have adventures like that. My sister never does. Your mamma never does. Only you and your great-aunt Wealthy. I don't want to spend my days doing laundry and my nights knitting or making lace. I want adventures! And I thought you did too."

"Nobody wants adventures like that one," Fan informed her. "I remember the bear—all teeth and horrid breath. And all Millie had was a parasol!"

Millie shivered. The parasol her Aunt Wealthy had given her had frightened the bear, but it was Bob-for-short, Fan's hound pup, who had saved them and given up his own life to do it. "I remember it," Fan said again, the corners of her sweet mouth turning down.

"Pish-tosh," said Millie, handing the completed garland to Annis. "I will still be myself, after all, even after I am wed. I have never lacked for adventure. Let's finish filling our buckets." She stood and pulled Jaz to her feet.

"I think getting married is scarier than fighting bears," Jaz said. "Are you taking your parasol with you?"

"Down the aisle? I don't think so. I doubt I shall need it at the altar."

"I'm glad she's getting married," Annis said. "Everyone in town thought that she would be an old maid forever. You have no idea, Millie, how hard it is to be the youngest sister of an old maid."

"Old maid!" Millie put her hands on her hips in mock anger. "Who says so?"

Fan started picking berries again and dropping them into her pail. "Mrs. Monocker said that it was a shame for someone as pretty as you to be an old maid."

Uncertainties

"Mrs. Prior said you could catch any man you wanted," Jaz agreed. "She said you were simply not applying yourself, and that was a sin and a shame."

"It certainly was neither a sin nor a shame," Millie said, turning pink. "It would have been a sin to apply myself to attracting young men I had no intention of keeping, and a shame to play with their hearts."

"I'm going to marry the first man who asks me," Annis said, putting her daisy chain on her head like a bridal wreath.

"You most certainly shall not," Millie said. "You only get one chance to choose a husband, Annis. Take your time and do it correctly."

"Widow Clark has chosen three times." Fan flicked a beetle from a leaf. "What I want to know is why she can't choose one who won't die of the cough or the shakes."

"Mr. Clark fell off a horse," Jaz pointed out. "He was healthy aside from that."

"Girls!" Millie said. "Mrs. Clark has had a very hard life, and Jesus' heart hurts for her. I am sure He would not want us to speak of her in such a manner."

"Sorry, Lord," Jaz waved at the sky, as if God were peeking at her from behind a cloud. "I am trying to learn to think before I speak. You know I am. But there is so much to think about that sometimes it just spills out."

Annis adjusted her garland. "I will marry my first beau. Pappa would never let an incorrect young man ask to be my beau. And if Pappa approved of him, he would be a fine young man."

"But what if *you* don't approve?" Jaz said, throwing a berry at her. "I'm sure I'm never going to approve of anyone, even if he begs for my hand."

Millie's Reluctant Sacrifice

Annis fell to her knees and clasped her hands in front of her, pretending to be a beau. "Miss Mikolaus," she said, "say you will marry me. If I do not hear words of love from those sweet lips, I shall…I shall die!"

"Expire," Jaz suggested. "It's much more romantic."

"I shall expire!" Annis looked mischievously through her lashes at Millie. "Did Charles say he would expire?"

"Certainly not," Millie said. "Now get up before you get grass stains on your skirt!"

Annis scrambled to her feet. "Gavriel said that Charles asked you to marry him over and over again."

"That's true." Millie reached up and hooked the handle of her parasol around a berry wand, pulling it down so the girls could reach the fat, ripe berries on the top. "He asked me the first time when I was sixteen years old."

Annis's eyes grew big. "That's six years ago!"

"I'm pleased to see that your sums are improving," Millie said. "Now let's see if your berry-picking skills can compare. Your pail is only half full."

"Six years!" Annis repeated. "Why, that's almost a decade! You were an infant!"

"I was sixteen," Millie said.

"Did he ask Pappa first?" Fan demanded. "I don't think Pappa would allow any of his daughters to marry at sixteen."

"I was living with Uncle Horace Dinsmore at Roselands for a year," Millie said. "So Charles could not talk to Pappa."

"Didn't you love him?" Annis asked.

"I did love him," Millie said, "from the first time he asked. But he did not know Jesus as his Lord."

"And Paul said not to be married to unbelievers," Fan said. "In Second Corinthians."

Uncertainties

"That's true." Millie set her pail down. "Ever since I was smaller than Annis, I have dreamed about my wedding day." She picked a flower from Annis's garland and held it in front of her. "I will stand beside the groom and say: 'Where you go I will go, and where you stay I will stay. Your people will be my people and your God my God. Where you die I will die, and there I will be buried.'"

"That's what Mamma said to Pappa when they married," Annis said. "And she had to follow him to Pleasant Plains, away from her home and dear Aunt Wealthy."

"I remember when Charles came to Pleasant Plains." Fan squinted as if it helped her see into the past. "It was the year of the big snow. The year you killed the bear. He prayed with us, and went to church. I'm sure he was a Christian by that time. Didn't he ask you then?"

"No," Millie said. "He had just lost his fortune and could not support a wife."

"Good thing he learned to be a doctor," Annis said. "Mrs. Prior says it's high time you settled down!"

"I think it's time we start home," Millie said. "Our pails are full, and I would like to stop at Celestia Ann's house."

"Oh, yes!" Annis said. "I want to play with the baby!"

Climbing roses covered the front porch of the small parsonage, their red and yellow blossoms shaded by a huge oak tree.

"Hullo, Mith Keith," a little girl called from the rope swing that hung from its branches. "Haf you come to thee the baby?"

"I came to see my favorite pupil," Millie said with a smile, "Miss Joy Everlasting Lord."

7

Millie's Reluctant Sacrifice

"Really? You came to thee me?" Joy Everlasting's face brightened. "Everyone elth comes to thee the baby."

Matthew Boone Lord, who was just four, nodded solemnly, his red curls bobbing around his ears.

"New visitors often get attention," Millie said.

"I don't think thee's vithiting," Joy Everlasting said. "Thee's been here five months already."

"I'm just starting a piecrust, Millie," Celestia Ann's voice called from the kitchen window. "Come on in."

The girls crowded into the tiny kitchen, and Millie was dismayed to see that Celestia Ann already had company. Fan's face contorted as if she had walked into a bad odor rather than into the company of an old friend. Millie made an effort to rearrange her own face into a smile.

"Helen! We were not expecting you," Millie said. "I hope we are not disturbing anything important?"

"Not at all," Celestia Ann said before Helen could speak. Helen Monocker's marriage to Mr. Grange's older brother had elevated her to a leading lady of society, and as such she felt it was her duty to instruct and set examples for those who were less fortunate than she was. She had made a special case of the pastor's wife.

"Don't track sand in!" Helen said sharply as Joy Everlasting and Matthew Boone came in the door. "It will grind the carpets!"

"Nonsense," Celestia Ann said with a smile. "I can always sweep when we are done visiting."

"We brought you blackberries," Annis said, holding up her pail.

"Now isn't that good timing!" Celestia Ann beamed at the little girl. "I will just have to make extra piecrusts! I was going to make apple pies, as I haven't time to gather berries myself."

8

"I cannot imagine why not!" Helen sniffed. "With a husband and three children to care for. The church pays Reverend Lord enough to hire a girl to help you, Celestia Ann. If you did not insist on feeding every hungry stranger who walks up to this door, you would have more than enough to pay for a servant."

"The Bible commands us to show hospitality," Celestia Ann said sweetly. "Some people have entertained angels without knowing it!"

Helen glanced around the small room. "I'm sure the angels have sense enough to go to houses that can afford to entertain them. If you want to know what I think, you and your husband show too much hospitality! It would be such a blessing to have a girl to help around here."

"She would have to sleep in the tree," Celestia Ann said with a laugh. "Our house is so full of blessings it's about to burst!"

Millie smiled as she leaned over the bassinet in the corner of the kitchen. The Lords' latest blessing, little Mary Grace, was fast asleep, her long, dark lashes brushing her cheeks. Millie put her finger to her lips, motioning for the girls to be quiet as they crowded around the bassinet.

"She is so adorable," Fan said. "Can we hold her, Celestia Ann? Please?"

"If you get her up now, she will be grumpy. Why don't you play with Joy and little Matthew while Millie and I visit? We will call you when she wakes." The girls looked disappointed.

"If you had an old quilt," Millie suggested, "you could turn the gorse bush by the gate into a teepee."

"I have just the quilt," Celestia Ann said, motioning with her chin to the chest by the foot of her bed. "It's brown like a buffalo hide."

Millie's Reluctant Sacrifice

"A bucket would make a good stool," Millie said.

"And the apple crate from the shed could be a table." Celestia Ann shrugged. "That is, if you want to have a house." Joy Everlasting was bouncing on her toes at the thought of sharing a game with the older girls, but Jaz was clearly not excited.

"Of course," Millie said, handing Jasmine her parasol, "you will need something with which to protect yourselves."

"I'd rather have a musket," Jaz said. "You never killed a bear with a parasol."

"If a bear shows up, you call my momma," Joy Everlasting said, grabbing Annis's hand and pulling her toward the door. "We'll have roast bear for supper!"

"Yeah!" Matthew Boone stomped his feet at the thought. "For supper!"

"Would you like to stay and help with the pies?" Millie asked Fan. Fan's eyes darted to Helen, and she shook her head and followed the others outside.

Helen sniffed. "You should have encouraged Fan to stay and help. If she did not want to make pies there are other chores. Idle hands are the devil's workshop." It did not seem to occur to Helen that her own hands were idle in her lap. She sat perched like a fashionable doll atop a kitchen stool.

"There's not enough room for three to work in this kitchen," Celestia Ann pointed out.

"Since there is no room in the kitchen, she could have been sent to…" Helen's eyes searched for any chore that Celestia Ann had neglected, but apparently she could find none. "…weeding the garden," she finished lamely.

"She's watching over my garden," Celestia Ann said, nodding at Joy Everlasting and little Matthew. "I'm growing little Lords. And they will have all of their lives to do chores. Let them play."

"Really, Celestia Ann, sometimes you are too heavenly minded. You need to be more practical," Helen said. "You have been married long enough to wear some of your idealism away! You must be practical, and demand that your husband be practical as well."

"I don't think we have been married nearly long enough for that," Celestia Ann said with a smile. She handed Millie an apron. Millie tied it around her waist and rolled up her sleeves.

"What's it like?" Millie asked as she dusted her hands with flour.

"The pie dough?" Celestia Ann winked. "A little dry. I think it needs some water."

"Don't tease," Millie said. "I meant marriage. What is it really like? Did you know that Matthew Lord was the right one for you before you wed?"

"The minute I laid eyes on that preacher man," Celestia Ann said, "with his bony wrists poking out of his too-short coat sleeves, I knew I had found my calling. A man of God should have sleeves of a proper length when he stands up to preach the Word."

"I still have questions about Joseph," Helen said, then looked surprised at her own words. Helen's marriage had been a social coup, a match with a very wealthy man. But Joseph was almost three times her age, and all the spark and excitement of life seemed to have worn off him, leaving him tired, though solid and temperate. "I mean, I do love him. I do!" She sounded as if she were trying to convince herself. "But I was so nervous when I walked down the aisle, I could hardly stand. Weren't you nervous, Celestia Ann?"

Millie's Reluctant Sacrifice

"Nope." Celestia Ann laid the pastry cloth across the table, and Millie sprinkled it with flour. The kitchen was beginning to warm up from the heat of the oven, and she wiped her forehead on her sleeve. "I worked so hard to catch him, I didn't have time to be nervous. Just glad. Are you nervous, Millie?"

Both of the older women stopped to look at her, and Millie felt the heat creep into her face. If there was a patent medicine to stop blushing, Millie would have bought it by the barrel. "I am, a little."

Helen nodded sympathetically.

"I do know he is the one for me," Millie hurried on. "But I had reconciled myself to being a spinster. I had my life all planned out. I was going to…"

"*Was going to* doesn't matter anymore," Helen said. "The responsibilities of a married woman will put an end to such childish things. The Bible says that a good wife is good to find, that she's God's gift to a man. But did you ever notice that it does not say a husband is good to find? It doesn't call a husband a gift, either."

Millie tried to keep the pity from her eyes, but it must have seeped in, for Helen cleared her throat before speaking. "Well. Enough of that. You haven't had time to order a wedding dress unless you have one already in your trousseau."

"I am making my own dress," Millie said. "It's almost finished. I had just received a bolt of pale blue georgette from my Aunt Wealthy when Charles proposed."

"Blue! No woman of fashion is married in blue. Not since Queen Victoria's wedding. She has made white the only color in which to be wed!"

"Queen Victoria will never have to wear her wedding dress again," Millie pointed out. "But I will be able to use mine over and over, with a different bodice, of course."

Uncertainties

"Millie Keith!" Helen's disapproval was clearly written on her face. "Frugality was understandable, even admirable, when you arrived in Pleasant Plains. We all knew that your family had reduced fortunes. And while society was perfectly willing to take this into consideration, the Keiths' fortunes have certainly turned around. Do you want your husband to be humiliated?"

"Blue will be lovely." Celestia Ann smiled at Millie, then turned to Helen, hands on her hips. "What on earth does the Queen of England have to do with the American frontier?"

"We are hardly the frontier anymore," Helen sniffed. "And it is fitting that we keep up with fashion."

"Millie will be in perfect fashion," Celestia Ann said. "Marry in white, you've chosen right; marry in blue, your love will be true; marry in red, wish yourself dead; marry in yel—"

"I may have a wedding shawl, as well," Millie said, quickly interrupting her friend. "Of darker blue."

Celestia Ann bit her lip. Helen had been married years before Queen Victoria had changed wedding fashions, and she had been lovely in yellow silk with green sprigs. But she certainly had not been thinking of old rhymes that ended with "marry in yellow, ashamed of the fellow," when she chose her gown.

"Blue will be lovely, I'm sure," Helen said stiffly. "I must be going. Mrs. Chetwood is coming to tea at four, and I must make sure that the tray is set. Good-bye, dear." She gave Celestia Ann's cheek a stiff kiss. "I will call again soon. There's no need to let me out. But do consider the matters we discussed earlier."

Millie and Celestia Ann watched through the window as Helen stopped to speak to the children by the teepee; then

13

Millie's Reluctant Sacrifice

Helen let herself out the gate, her shoulders drooping with the weight of bringing culture and fashion to the backward town of Pleasant Plains.

Celestia Ann shook her head and sighed. "Helen is very good for my prayer life," she said. "And for that I am thankful. How is your prayer life, Millie?" There was mischief in her voice and a twinkle in her eye. "It's only a few weeks until the wedding!"

"It has all happened so quickly. I feel as if I am living in a dream," Millie said honestly.

"You always have been a dreamer."

"That's true," Millie said. "But I've always had my feet on the ground, even when my head was in the clouds. And now…"

"Your feet are in the clouds and your head is on the ground?" Celestia Ann laughed. "Haven't you been praying for Charles Landreth for years?"

"Yes," Millie said. "I prayed for him every day, and missed him horribly. I read the entries in my journal, but the words simply do not reflect the real emotion. It was an ache that cannot be described."

"Millie Keith, don't you know by now that God answers prayer."

"I do. I still almost fainted when he appeared on the porch."

"You? Faint?" Celestia Ann laughed. "I'd like to see that."

"Seriously," Millie said. "It's like a fairy tale, but a very confusing one. You know I have been called into foreign missions." Celestia Ann nodded. She was the only friend Millie had told about her call. "I have been preparing myself for that very thing, and suddenly my own Prince Charming walks through the front door."

Uncertainties

"Only..." Celestia Ann raised her eyebrows.

"Only he's on the wrong page!" Millie sighed. "Helen can't be right, can she? Marriage won't mean the end of God's call on my life, will it?"

"Of course not," Celestia Ann said. "Not if you are marrying the right man. Why would you even think such a thing?"

"Because..." Millie glanced out the window to make sure the girls were not listening. "Because I have neglected to tell Charles that we are going to China!"

CHAPTER

Certain Assurances

*For your Father knows what
you need before you
ask him.*

MATTHEW 6:8

*C*elestia Ann stopped rolling the dough. "You haven't told Charles?"

"I know what you're thinking," Millie said. "But honestly, this has all happened so suddenly. He was only here for a few days, before he returned to Chicago to set things in order. He had to make sure his patients were in good hands."

"But haven't you written letters? It's been two months!"

"I...I tried. But it seems like the kind of thing I should tell him face-to-face."

"Millie, if Charles Landreth hasn't heard the call to missions—"

"Of course he has," Millie said. "He must have forgotten to mention it as well. Perhaps he was so sure of it that he felt it did not bear mentioning."

"Perhaps pigs will fly. Millie, you have got to talk..."

Mary Grace sneezed and started to whimper. "Not yet, sweetie," Celestia Ann said softly. "Mamma's got her hands in the pie!"

"I'll change her." Millie scooped the baby up, glad for an excuse to change the subject, if not the nappy. A tickle of panic had been growing inside her with each letter she wrote to Charles. She had tried to find the words, but ended by wadding up each and every attempt. "Dearest, I know I should have mentioned this earlier, but how do you feel about going to the mission field in China?"

Of course Celestia Ann is right, Lord. I should have spoken to Charles about it before he returned to Chicago, she prayed as she laid Mary Grace on the changing blanket. *But I didn't, and now I need Your help.* Mary Grace kicked and cooed, glad to be rid of the wet diaper. Millie tucked the new one under her and tied it in place. *Your call to me was so clear. Please speak to Charles as well.*

Millie recalled the monumental moment when she heard God's call to foreign missions. A traveling missionary was in Pleasant Plains and Millie had attended the meetings. On one occasion, the missionary began to describe an orphanage in the city of Peking. As Millie listened to the missionary's description of the poor living conditions of the orphanage and the need for Christians to pray for those lonely children, Millie's heart began to break. *And then it happened!* Millie said to herself as she remembered. *I heard a voice in my heart! It said, "They need to know Jesus. Tell them."* At that moment, Millie had looked around quickly to see if any of the other ladies had heard the command, but not even Celestia Ann had seemed aware of the strange vibration in the air. It had been enough to change the course of Millie's life. *That's when I knew I was called to foreign missions. The Holy Spirit spoke to me as clearly as if He'd spoken aloud. I just know it was You, Lord!*

"And God can be just as clear with Charles, can't He?" Millie said to Mary Grace as she patted the baby's tummy. Mary Grace cooed back at her and smiled. "Of course He can," Millie said while the tiny hand grabbed her finger. "He is the God of details, after all. Look what a good job He did on you! If the Lord Himself brought us together after so many years, His hand must be in it. But—" Millie picked the baby up and whispered in her ear, "I'm just a teeny bit worried, Mary Grace. Promise you won't tell a soul!"

Mary Grace laughed and grabbed Millie's braid.

"She's awake!" Annis had seen them through the bedroom window. "Why didn't you call us?"

Certain Assurances

Millie carried the baby back into the kitchen just as Annis burst through the door, with the others behind her. Jaz had stained her cheeks with berry juice stripes, and had twigs sticking out from her hair. "We intend to raise her in the ways of the Potawatami tribe!" she declared.

"And feed her lizards," Matthew Boone said, "to make her brave!"

"The Potawatami did not eat lizards," Celestia Ann said.

"What did they eat?" the little boy asked.

"Well, when they visited our cabin," Celestia Ann said, "they liked to have berry tarts and tea."

"I want berry tarts!" Matthew Boone cried.

"And you will have some, if you promise to take good care of your little sister. Will you take a blanket out for her, Millie? I'll be out as soon as the pies and tarts are in the oven," Celestia Ann said. "This kitchen is so hot, they might bake on the table top!"

Millie carried the blanket outside and laid it in the shade not too far from the porch, while the tribe of children gathered around the baby protectively. Mary Grace loved the attention, kicking her heels and squealing with delight. Millie sat in the porch rocker where she could keep a close eye on them all.

"When does Charles arrive?" Celestia Ann asked when she joined Millie at last.

"In two weeks. The wedding is in three, and that's almost too soon. My dress is nearly finished, but the girls' dresses are not." She was sure Celestia Ann knew she did not want to discuss China in front of the girls.

"Adah is helping?" Celestia Ann asked, and Millie sighed with relief.

"In her own way. Adah is of the belief that the need for pins, needles, and thread were the result of the fall of man at worst, and merely a way to keep girls from studying books at best. But if she did not read to us, the tatting, knitting, and sewing every evening would be very dull. And Zillah is so clever with her needle that she does the work of two. Wallace has been kind enough to allow her to spend her evenings with us for the last few weeks."

They talked of sewing and bridal cake recipes until their noses informed them that the tarts were done. Millie watched over the children while Celestia Ann took the tarts from the oven and put in the pies. It gave Millie time to think—time for the worries to come back. *Will my wedding dress be fine enough to suit Charles? Called into missions or not, he is still a doctor. Am I ready to be a doctor's wife?*

"You had no doubts that you were called to be a pastor's wife?" Millie asked when Celestia Ann sat down again after distributing the tarts to the hungry tribe of children.

"I didn't say that." Celestia Ann dimpled. "I knew I wanted to be Matthew's wife. But when it came time to say 'I do,' I doubted I could stand up, I was shaking so hard—don't let the baby off the blanket!"

Mary Grace was kicking like a frog, scooting herself toward the plate of tarts.

"She's a Wap-up-ona-onami!" Matthew Boone said proudly, pulling her back onto the blanket by one leg.

"I guess it's time I take the rest of these Potawatami home," Millie said, giving her friend a hug. "Mamma will want to put up the berries tonight." She gathered her bonnet and parasol, kissed Mary Grace and Joy Everlasting good-bye, and helped fold the teepee, while Jaz tried to wash the war paint from her face at the backyard pump. The little girl managed to distribute the color more evenly, at least giving her an all-over blush.

"That will have to do," Millie decided at last. "Any more scrubbing and your face might come off."

"Take one of these pies home with you," Celestia Ann said. "Let me wrap it in a towel."

"Mith Keith?" Joy Everlasting looked at her with huge eyes. "Mithus Helen says that you won't teach uth piano anymore after you get married. Ith that true?"

"I am not certain," Millie said. "But if I do give up my music school, Effie Prescott will take my students, and she is a very good teacher."

"I like you better," Joy Everlasting said.

"Thank you, dear," Millie said. "But I'm sure you will love Miss Effie just as much, once you get to know her."

"Here you go," Celestia Ann said, holding out the towel-wrapped pie. "And Millie, promise me you will speak to Charles as soon as he arrives."

"I promise." *Celestia Ann is right. I do have to talk with Charles as soon as possible. As soon as we can sit down face-to-face.*

~

The garden gate complained loudly as Annis pulled it open, a reminder that Rupert Keith had spent the summer as an assistant to a pharmacist near his college. It was a great opportunity, but the whole farm missed him, with fences drooping and the barn shedding shingles like tears. The hinges on the gate complained of his absence most loudly. Stuart Keith had spoken many times of hiring a handyman, but it had not happened, and Keith Hill creaked and groaned for Ru's return. Don and Cyril had spent the summer at school as well. Don's advanced course was only an excuse not to leave his twin, who was spending the summer with tutors so as not to be left behind in the fall term. Keith Hill was far too quiet without the three brothers.

"Ah, the berry pickers," Stuart Keith said as he opened the door. "And what is this? Marcia!" he called over his shoulder to his wife. "Perhaps we should raise the bride price that young man is paying. Our Millie's more amazing than the maiden who spins straw into gold! Here we send her for berries, and she returns with a pie!"

"Silly Pappa," Annis said, tugging at his hand. "We stopped at Celestia Ann's house."

"Oh, that explains it." He swung her up till her boots almost touched the ceiling.

"You are home early," Millie said, kissing his cheek.

"Mr. Ormsby is holding down the fort at the law office. I thought I might like to spend the afternoon with my lovely wife. Why don't you let me take that pie? I'll put it some-where safe."

"In your stomach?" Annis asked.

"That would be very safe," he said, reaching for the pie plate.

"Stuart!" Marcia said, "We will have it after dinner." Marcia Keith's face had been etched by smiles over the years, and her hair was now more grey than blonde, but her eyes were still young.

"If I must give up the pie," he sighed, "I should be able to see what is in the package, at least."

"What package, Pappa?"

"And a letter as well, both for Miss Millie Keith!" The letter was from Charles, and this Millie tucked into her apron pocket, but the package had come from Aunt Wealthy Stanhope in Ohio.

"It's books, of course," Stuart said.

24

Certain Assurances

Millie cut the twine and unwrapped a handsome three-volume set. "You are practically a prophet, Pappa," she said, holding up the first volume. "*The Commander's Account of a Naval Exploration* by Captain Robert FitzRoy. And the note says, 'Dear Millie, Allow me to be the first to contribute to the merging libraries of M. Keith and C. Landreth. I found these books both excellent and informative, but too heavy to carry with me on the stage.' Mamma, Aunt Wealthy will be here on Saturday's stage! She says nothing else, but sends her love."

"Of course, she will," Marcia said. "We need her help with the wedding cake, and that alone will take a week! Now bring those berries into the kitchen, girls. You can help make berry preserves."

Millie left the books in the parlor while she helped her mother and sisters, first with preparing the berries and then with supper. Charles's letter rested like a promise in her apron pocket all afternoon and into the evening. She was tempted to read it while her sisters sewed, but resisted the urge. The dresses had to be done, and the quicker each seam was finished, the quicker she would be able to read.

The candles had burned to stubs before Millie said good night to her family, took her new books, and climbed the stairs to her bedroom. The private library of M. Keith almost filled two shelves above her writing desk. She could just fit Captain FitzRoy's books on the second shelf, next to *A Lady's Adventures in the Orient*, *Missionary Travels in China*, and *The Care and Tending of Sheep in China*. This last had been far from fascinating in style or content. Keith Hill had never had a herd of sheep, and after reading the book, Millie was rather glad of it.

Millie's Reluctant Sacrifice

She lit her desk lamp and pulled Charles's letter from her pocket. *Dearest*—the word made Millie smile every time she read it—*I have had excellent news. Otis is going to be my best man!* This was good news and Millie was happy for him. Except for Otis and old Mrs. Travilla, Charles had been disowned by his friends and family in the South. He had lived in Chicago as a stranger in a strange land during the years of medical school and starting a practice. *He will be traveling to Pleasant Plains and may arrive before I do. Mrs. Travilla sends her best wishes and her love, but is not able to travel. She is joining me in prayers for Otis's salvation. If I could snatch my friends from the fire, he would be the first....*

Millie read the letter through twice, then folded it carefully and set it in the tin box that held every letter he had ever written her. There had not been one word about missions, or even China, in any of them. *What if Charles is not called...?* She could not get Celestia Ann's words out of her mind. *Can I be content as just a doctor's wife?*

Millie knelt by her bed, her head bowed in silent prayer for Charles, for Otis, and finally for herself. Then she opened her Bible to Psalm 127.

> *Unless the Lord builds the house,*
> *its builders labor in vain.*
> *Unless the Lord watches over the city,*
> *the watchmen stand guard in vain.*
> *In vain you rise early*
> *and stay up late,*
> *toiling for food to eat —*
> *for he grants sleep to those he loves.*

Certain Assurances

Millie pulled on her nightgown and slipped into bed. *Lord*, she prayed, *You be the one to build our life together. You be the Builder of our lives.*

⁓

"Millie! Have you seen Adah?"

Millie turned from the mirror where she was adjusting her cap and smiled at her mother. "Not since breakfast."

"She must be in the loft," Stuart said, standing on tiptoe so that he could see in the mirror over Millie's head.

"And not dressed for town?" Marcia exclaimed.

"With hay sticking from her ears. Aunt Wealthy won't mind a button or a fig," Stuart said with a laugh, "but her sister Zillah will. How is she ever going to find a husband for Adah if the girl will not cooperate?"

"Zillah's matchmaking can wait a few years," Marcia said. "Adah is only eighteen."

"Now, now. Zillah only wants happiness for her sister," Stuart said. "Newlyweds always want everyone else to be in love as well. You've made one sister very happy, Millie."

"Now I must find the other and make her unhappy by hauling her away from her books." Millie gave her cap a final pat and hurried through the back door. Chicks scattered before her as she crossed the hen yard, careful to hold the hem of her skirt clear of the dust.

"Adah!" Millie called, but there was no reply. Millie pulled off her lace gloves and tucked them into her sash before she entered the barn and started up the wooden ladder to the loft. She paused at the top and shook her head.

Adah was framed in the golden glow of a sunbeam, obviously absorbed in the book she held on her lap. She was still

Millie's Reluctant Sacrifice

wearing the simple housedress she had worn to breakfast, and her nut-brown hair was pulled back in a loose bun.

"Adah! Don't you want to go with us to greet Aunt Wealthy?"

Adah jumped up, clutching the book to her breast. "Is it time already? I thought I would just read for a few moments after breakfast—"

"It's almost noon," Millie said, picking a stray straw from her sister's hair. "Everyone else is dressed. You must come as you are. There's no time to change now."

Adah's face fell, and Millie repented of her harsh tone. Adah was a dreamer, it was true, but the kind of dreamer Millie was sure was close to God's heart, for all of her dreams were of good and honorable things. "Never mind. Aunt Wealthy will be happy to see you no matter what you are wearing."

The stagecoach was waiting in the yard, and Stuart handed in first Adah and then Millie, where they settled beside Marcia, Fan, and Annis.

Zillah was at the station when they arrived, holding on to the arm of her young husband. Zillah had made an excellent choice in Wallace Ormsby, and she now dressed and acted every inch the young lawyer's wife.

"Adah! You should take more care in your appearance!" she scolded. "You never know who will be on that stage. Eligible young men are few and far between, and you only have one chance to make a first impression."

"I'm not looking for a young man," Adah said. "Or an old one, either. I'm quite happy with my studies and my books."

"Fan!" Marcia caught the sash of the girl's apron as she headed for the stables. "Stay on the boardwalk until Aunt Wealthy arrives. I don't want your pantalets getting wet."

Certain Assurances

Fan looked longingly across the muddy stable yard to where Gordon Lightcap, the owner of the stage station, and his brother-in-law, Jedidiah Mikolaus, were finishing shoveling out the stalls. The Lightcaps and Keiths were as close as family to one another. Fan spent as much time helping Jed with the horses as Jasmine spent with Annis.

"Open the stable doors, Jed," Gordon said, checking his pocket watch. "The stage is coming." At that moment, the stagecoach bugle blared, announcing that the stage was rounding the bend in the road.

"I'm going to see her first!" Annis said, leaning out so far that Millie had to pull her back. The horses reared as the stage jolted to a stop. The driver leaped to the ground, and Jedidiah took the horses by the harness while Gordon stepped up to open the stagecoach door.

Two ladies and one gentleman exited the stage, stretching and rubbing their backs. Fan and Annis stood on tiptoe trying to see around them. Next, a large lady hesitated in the door, seeming to fill it as completely as a cork fills a bottleneck. Gordon took her hand and pulled gently until she popped out, then steadied her as she tottered toward the station. Before he could turn back, a tiny lady in a purple travel dress and a feathered turban appeared and hopped to the ground.

"Aunt Wealthy!" Annis squealed.

"Aunt Wealthy!" Stuart kissed her cheek. "I would have helped you down."

"Pish-tosh," Aunt Wealthy said. "I am quite capable of exiting a stage."

Jaz was looking at her wide-eyed. "She's carrying her umbrella," she whispered, as if it were the grail from King Arthur's tales.

Aunt Wealthy disappeared in a swarm of eager nieces and friends, from which she emerged with her turban askew and her eyes a-twinkle. "Goodness! It's almost worth going away, just to be greeted when I return!"

Aunt Wealthy's trunks were loaded on a wagon which was to be driven by Jedidiah. Fan and Annis begged to be allowed to ride with him, and after making sure their bonnets were tied, Marcia agreed. The welcoming party started home, having grown from one coach to a caravan of coach, surrey, and wagon. People waved and called greetings as they passed through the town.

"My, Pleasant Plains has grown!" Aunt Wealthy said as they crossed the town square. "It isn't the frontier any longer, is it?"

"That's the problem with the frontier," Stuart Keith sighed. "If you want to live on it, you have to keep moving. We are positively civilized around here these days, Wealthy."

When they reached Keith Hill, Stuart and Wallace carried Wealthy's trunks to Zillah's old room, the guest room having been set aside for Charles. Jedidiah helped Millie and Fan put away the coach and surrey teams before he turned the wagon back to the stagecoach station. Aunt Wealthy was given the royal tour, which included the conservatory that had been added for Millie's music school, and the new carriage house that stood beyond the barn.

"The Lord is so good," Aunt Wealthy said when they were settled in the Keiths' kitchen at last. "I knew that He was calling you to Pleasant Plains, but I hardly thought that He would give you so much. Do you remember the big yellow house you first lived in here? And the furniture made of boxes? And how is that lovely minister, Reverend

Almighty doing?" Aunt Wealthy asked. "Do you remember the day he sat on the furniture tacks?"

The next hour was filled with "do you remembers" and laughter, while Marcia and Millie prepared the evening meal.

"Now tell me all about the boys," Aunt Wealthy said when they sat down to eat at last. "It seems far too quiet around here without them. They are coming home for the wedding?"

"They will just have time before the fall term starts," Millie said. "That is why we planned the wedding so soon. I couldn't bear not to have them, and couldn't bear to wait until next summer, either."

"It will be so good to see them," Marcia sighed. "It is hard to let them go."

"Now, dear," Stuart said. "You know school is the best thing for them. We prayed about it—"

"I know it is best for them," Marcia agreed. "But it's hard on me."

"Rather hard on the school as well, I understand," said Wallace as he passed a plate of brown biscuits to his wife.

"Cyril was not at fault in the fire," Millie said quickly. "He had nothing to do with it."

"A case could be made," Wallace said. "He did, after all, put a dead cat under the floorboards of that boy's room. Without the smell, fumigation would not have been tried."

"Ahem."

"I apologize, Stuart," Wallace said. "Ladies. That is hardly delicate conversation for mealtime."

Millie was glad the conversation had changed course. Wallace Ormsby had a keen legal mind, but he did not understand Cyril at all. And while she knew it was quite wrong to have a favorite little brother, Millie had spent a great deal of time praying for Cyril. *He has been trying so hard since he gave his heart to the Lord. And wasn't the great apostle Paul something of a troublemaker as well?*

"Annabeth, Beatrice, and Camilla send their love," Aunt Wealthy said, then covered her mouth with her hand as Millie's eyes filled with a sudden sting of tears.

"It's all right," Millie said. "It's been four years, and none of us can seem to remember that Annabeth is gone. How is Frank?"

"Hasn't his letter come? Frank received your invitation and will be here for the wedding. Little Frank as well. He is completely devoted to his son and wouldn't think of leaving him."

"Hasn't he remarried?" Wallace asked. "Raising a child on his own!"

Aunt Wealthy shook her head. "Half the young women of Lansdale think the young pastor would be a marvelous catch. But Frank seems to have no interest in remarrying. He is satisfied with his studies and his sermons."

"We can put them in with Ru," Marcia said happily. "Keith Hill will be bursting at the seams!"

When the meal was over, Stuart and Wallace excused themselves to the front porch to talk, while the ladies made short work of the dishes.

"Enough of that!" Aunt Wealthy said, when the last dish was dried and put away. "Now let's have a look at this gown you have written me about. I hardly thought that bolt of fabric would be made into a wedding dress!"

Millie led the way up the stairs, and they all crowded into her room.

"I see your trousseau is in a travel trunk," Aunt Wealthy said with a nod of approval as Millie started to unbuckle the heavy straps. "Very practical."

"I don't want a travel trunk," Annis said. "I want a trousseau like Lu's! She has lace flounces, ball dresses from Paris, dresses for breakfast and dinner, dresses for receptions and parties…"

"Her lace flounces alone cost more than Keith Hill," Zillah said. "So you had best set your sights a little lower."

Millie took out her wedding dress. The blue georgette had been the perfect fabric for the pattern she had chosen. The skirt was full, and she had added a scalloped hem that showed a flash of pantalets and lace at her ankle. With the bodice she had been more elaborate, adding fourteen crochet buttons down the back, a demi-shawl that ruffled slightly over each shoulder, and a high collar of Irish lace.

"The color matches your eyes exactly!" Aunt Wealthy said, when Millie held it up. "I thought that it would! And it will set off your golden hair, as well."

"You don't think it's too simple?" Millie couldn't help but ask.

"My dear," Marcia said, hanging it on the back of Millie's door, "simple can be very elegant. Especially when the soul inside is adorned with the unfading beauty of a gentle and quiet spirit, as our beloved Lord desires."

Millie laid her carefully sewn garments on the bed one by one. Aunt Wealthy examined each item as a chef might consider another cook's meal, testing the fabric with her fingers and feeling the seams. Millie handed them to her one at a time: a walking dress, three day dresses, two nightgowns, three petticoats, three pairs of drawers, two chemises, and two dozen pair of plain stockings. Finally, from the bottom of the trunk, a pair of new brogans, suitable for walking the mountains of China.

Millie's Reluctant Sacrifice

"Lovely!" Aunt Wealthy said at last, and Millie felt a flash of pride. They were simple garments, it was true, made from fabrics that would wear well, but she had taken special care with their fitting, and where her needle could add a trace of elegance or style she had not spared the labor. "And practical as well. I notice that you still have room, and not surprisingly so, as this marriage has come upon you suddenly. I brought several things that you might like to add. If Annis and Adah would help me carry a few packages from my room?"

The "few packages" filled the girls' arms and the room with excitement when they were piled on the bed.

"Aunt Wealthy!" Millie said, looking at the small mountain of gifts. "You shouldn't have!"

"Pish-tosh," Aunt Wealthy said. "If I shouldn't, I wouldn't. But I did."

"Open them, Millie!" Annis was dancing with impatience.

There were travel dresses in black silk, pongee, and pique; a heavy wool cape, two party dresses, real lace handkerchiefs, satin dancing slippers, and several smart bonnets. Each item was exclaimed over and passed from hand to hand to be examined as Millie dug deeper into the mountain of fabric.

"How could you have done all this sewing?" Millie asked at last.

"The needlework is courtesy of the Ladies Society of Lansdale. They meet at my house, you know. We've had two months to work, and in two months we could clothe an army."

"It's too much!" Millie said as Aunt Wealthy handed her one last package. She untied the strings, opened the paper, and lifted out a veil of Spanish lace.

Certain Assurances

"Aunt Wealthy!" Marcia gasped. "It's exquisite! Where did you get it?"

"In New Orleans," Aunt Wealthy said. "Four years ago. I set it away for Millie's wedding. I had faith and certain assurances from the Lord that she would need it one day."

"It's time for Annis to go to bed," Marcia said as Millie began to repack her trunk.

"But Mamma!" cried Annis.

"Aunt Wealthy will be here tomorrow," Marcia said, taking her youngest daughter by the hand. "And many days thereafter. And you don't want to be too sleepy for Sunday school tomorrow."

"I hear that Millie teaches your class," Aunt Wealthy said. "And I was wondering if I might be your guest?"

"Yes!" Annis said, without looking to Millie.

"Well, then. I'd better get to bed myself, if we must wake up early," said Aunt Wealthy.

As Millie packed her trousseau garments away, she kept the wedding veil for last, running her fingers over it as she placed it in the trunk. *Certain assurances from the Lord,* she thought with a smile.

CHAPTER 3

An Early Arrival

*But as for me, I watch in hope
for the Lord, I wait for God
my Savior; my God will
hear me.*

MICAH 7:7

An Early Arrival

*A*lthough the clouds promised yet another rainy day, the Keiths chose to walk to services together the next morning, Marcia and Stuart hand in hand, followed by Fan, Adah, and Annis, with Millie and Aunt Wealthy bringing up the rear. The church served by Reverend Lord had grown almost too large for its small building, but they managed somehow to make room for each new person, making them feel as if they belonged. Millie left her parents at the door and followed Annis and Aunt Wealthy to the young ladies' Sunday school room.

"Good morning!" Aunt Wealthy said after Millie introduced her. The room of little girls in their starched and pressed Sunday-best stared at the little woman. Those who had not met Wealthy Stanhope in person had heard stories of her adventures, and Millie thought for a moment that they would be too shy to speak.

Finally Jaz cleared her throat. "Good morning, Miss Stanhope," she said, and the others joined in. "Did you know my Granmarie?" Jasmine asked when the chorus of good mornings was done. "My sister says you did."

"Yes, I did know your grandmother, a long time ago in Philadelphia, and you are a great deal like her. She was a very beautiful young woman."

Runhilda Ransquate raised her hand, and Millie smiled. Years ago, Runhilda's mother, Damaris Drybread, had been one of Millie's first and hardest-won friends in Pleasant Plains. Now Millie could not help but love Runhilda, the living proof of God's grace in her friend's life. "Mrs....Miss..." Runhilda flushed. "What is...Why are you a *Miss* Stanhope?"

"Runhilda!" Millie said.

"Never mind," Aunt Wealthy said. "I believe in questions. In fact, these young ladies can ask me anything at all, and I will do my best to answer. I am a Miss because I never married."

"So you are an old maid. My mother used to be one," Runhilda said, looking from side to side as if daring anyone to disagree. "Father says so, but she won't tell me what it was like."

"Well!" Aunt Wealthy folded her hands in her lap. "I can tell you what it is like for me. It says in the Bible that an unmarried woman is free to devote herself to God, and I have found that this is true."

"But weren't you ever in love?" Annis asked. All of the little girls leaned forward at this.

"Yes," Aunt Wealthy said. "Twice."

"Twice!" Jasmine shook her head as if to say this was not possible.

Aunt Wealthy dimpled at her. "My first love's name was Rob. He was a dashing fellow, but much older than me. I used to think I could run away with him and live in the forest."

"In the forest?"

"Yes, but he had a lady love named Marion."

"You mean Robin Hood! You can't fall in love with a character in a book," Jaz said in disgust.

"You are quite right, Jasmine," Aunt Wealthy said with a laugh, "but I was ten, and I certainly thought I was in love. He seemed so perfect. Dashing and handsome."

"But he wasn't real."

"That's what made him so easy to dream about. He was never cross or ill. He never had gravy stains on his shirt. Real people aren't like that at all, of course. Not one of the boys I knew could compare to him. But it can't be real love unless you truly know the person, and they know you as well. Nonetheless, I am still very fond of the color green."

At the mention of Robin Hood and the color green, Millie smiled inside and her thoughts drifted to Laylie and her "Merry Men." *I wonder how she is?* Millie thought. *Lord, would You send a special blessing to Laylie and her Merry Men today?*

"You said you were in love twice," Annis said, folding her arms. "Was the next love in a book as well?"

"Oh, no. My next love was a young man named Roger Jones." A small smile played on her lips, as if she were remembering something very sweet. "He was as handsome as King David, and quite a dancer as well. Beneath the gravy stains on his shirt beat a heart as bold as Lancelot's!"

"Did you ever kiss him?" asked Annis.

Millie opened her mouth to rebuke her sister, but said nothing. *Aunt Wealthy did say that any questions were welcomed*, Millie thought, shaking her head from side to side.

"In fact," Wealthy adjusted her cap, "I did. When he asked me to marry him." Wealthy glanced at Millie. Millie had lived with Wealthy for four years, and had never heard a word of an engagement. "Millie dear, a lady should never gape," said Wealthy.

The little girls giggled, and Millie shut her mouth.

"My parents believed I was too young to marry," Aunt Wealthy said. "And they were right. Roger went to the mission field. We wrote letters, of course. I still have them, every one. But Roger was killed just days before he was to set sail back to the United States for our wedding. I had already sewn my wedding gown."

"Oh, Miss Stanhope!" Jaz said. "I had no idea that your life had been touched by such tragedy!"

Millie's Reluctant Sacrifice

"Tragedy? Pish-tosh," Aunt Wealthy said. "My life was touched by great love. Love is never a tragedy—it is the victory. And the gown certainly wasn't wasted. I had a gown but no groom, and one day I met a bride with no gown. She wore the dress, and it was a great blessing to us both. One of these days, I will see Roger again, and we will have such a good time discussing our adventures."

"But to lose your true love…" Annis said.

"My dear," Aunt Wealthy said gently, "you can't imagine that you can keep anyone forever? Not on this earth. Every single day with someone you love is a gift, and should be lived just that way. But the only one who will be with you always is our Lord Jesus." Aunt Wealthy's eyes twinkled as she looked out over the room. "What would you say if I told you someone had written a love letter to you? Someone who knows you very, very well?" The girls looked at one another.

"It's true," Aunt Wealthy said as she looked at each of them. "God has written you a love letter, and it's called the Bible. You are His beloved." She rested her hand on Runhilda's shoulder. "His beautiful one. Just listen to how much He loves you." She opened her Bible and began to read. "For God so loved the world that he gave his one and only Son, that whoever believes in him shall not perish."

Millie settled into her seat and listened to Aunt Wealthy tell the story of the great Lover who gave His life to save His beloved. The girls listened as if they had never heard it before, and strangely, it seemed new to Millie as well, as if her love for Charles had somehow given her new understanding of how hard it must have been for the Father to send His Son to die. *You can't imagine you can keep anyone forever. Lord, help me to see each day with Charles as a gift from You.*

An Early Arrival

The mood followed Millie home from church, and she couldn't shake it even after having lunch. Finally, she put on her riding skirt and a matching cap and jacket that always made her feel pretty, and went to the barn to find Inspiration. The mare was as eager as Millie to head for the edges of the wilderness. The morning clouds had joined into a late afternoon greyness that stretched from horizon to horizon and promised an evening drizzle. Millie gave Inspiration the reins, and the mare set out in a long-legged stride toward the open spaces. Millie loved the solitude. It was times like these when God's presence was so close that she felt that if she turned quickly enough, she would see Him standing there, laughing.

Of course I cannot keep Charles forever. It will be wonderful enough to keep him for a time, and to have someone with whom to journey through life. Suddenly, a mourning dove exploded from the brush at Inspiration's feet and the horse shied. Millie patted her neck, coming back to the present. The air was thick and electric, reminding Millie that she should have started home long ago.

"I feel it, girl," she said. "We'll head home, and you will be in the nice safe barn before—" At that moment the storm announced its intentions with a brilliant bolt of lightning and an instant roar of thunder.

Inspiration exploded into a run. Millie leaned close to her neck to avoid the low branches, until she could finally calm the panicked horse. The thunder grumbling in the distance made Inspiration tremble, but her ears were cocked back toward the sound of Millie's soothing voice. The rain came around them like a wet, grey blanket, shrouding the trees and bushes. Millie's cap kept it from her eyes, but it drooped dismally, flopping down on her face. They had

Millie's Reluctant Sacrifice

travelled much farther than Millie had intended, and she was thoroughly wet and miserable. The wall of the storm, with its hot bolts of lightning, seemed to have passed them by, but she still spoke soothingly to Inspiration each time the horse tensed at the distant thunder's rumble.

"It's all right. We're going home now, and as soon as we are on the road, you will be able to run." The downpour showed no sign of easing. Instead, it seemed to draw the evening up out of the ground, shadows rising to meet shadows and forming an early dusk. The road was hardly visible in the drizzle of rain. Inspiration nodded her head and whickered, eager for the warm, safe barn.

"All right, girl," Millie said, easing the reins. "You can run." It took the mare only two jumps to hit her stride, and then she stretched into a full run, head down and nose toward Keith Hill. Millie leaned close against her neck again, this time to keep the stinging rain from her eyes.

Suddenly a shadow moved in the road ahead of them, and they were upon it before Millie realized it was a man. She reined left, but not quickly enough. Inspiration's shoulder caught him hard enough to send him sprawling. Millie pulled the horse to a stop, leaped from the saddle, and twisted Inspiration's reins around a branch before running back down the road. *Lord*, she prayed, *don't let him be hurt!*

At least the man had not lost his senses. He rolled over and sat up, reaching for the hat which floated beside him in the puddle.

"I am so sorry," Millie said. "This is such a lonely stretch of road, and I was trying to get home —"

"You have always been fond of making dramatic appearances, Miss Keith."

"Charles!"

44

An Early Arrival

"In the flesh, with the bruises to prove it." Charles Landreth's incredible smile flashed through the mud on his face.

"Charles!" Millie reached out to help him, but he waved her hand away and stood up.

"I'm quite all right, my dear." He stood and took a slow, deep breath. "Nothing broken."

"What are you doing here?" Millie stepped toward him, but he backed away holding his hands up.

"Now, Millie, I'm covered with mud. Head to foot. You will ruin your dress."

"Will you be still!" Millie said. "I don't care about my dress! I want to know that you are all right, and you are forcing me to chase you all over the road!"

"I'm fit as a ugggg…" he groaned. Millie jumped the puddle and wrapped her arms around him. "Well, that's settled then. The gown is spoiled, but it isn't my fault." He wrapped his arms around her in return. "What do you know? I feel better already! Ouch," he winced as she felt his ribs. "Gently, gently!"

"You are hurt!"

"I'm feeling much better than I was a few moments ago."

"What was wrong?" Millie asked, looking at him more closely.

"Nothing a brisk massage by a horse followed by a mud bath has not cured!" he said. "Would you be so kind as to pick up my hat?"

"But what are you doing here now?" Millie asked, once she was sure his arms and legs were still attached and in working order. "We weren't expecting you for a week!"

"I could not stand another moment without you. So I boarded a stage. The road is completely washed out between here and Riceville, and the stage had to turn back. I decided that ten miles was not too far to walk to see the one I love. It has taken me a bit longer than I anticipated, however. I thought I could make it to Keith Hill and be sitting in your parlor by now."

"It's not far," Millie said. "Inspiration can carry us both."

"Your horse?"

"Yes, of course," Millie said. "What other horse could I mean?"

"The one you tied to that bush?"

The bush was still where Millie had left it, but Inspiration was not. The small branch she had wrapped the reins around was snapped. "She's gone home," Millie said. "She has not been able to stand thunder since the tornado."

Charles started to laugh. "I have a confession to make," he said. "I was lost. I thought I knew this area well, but the last time I was here it was covered in snow. I turned left at the crossroads, and was just starting to believe I had made a wrong turn when you came along. You are an answer to prayer, my dear. You seem to have made it a habit to come to my rescue."

Millie could not help but laugh with him. She attempted a curtsey, but her skirts were too wet to cooperate, so she managed a soggy bob instead.

"Any time, sir. But I hardly see that it is a habit."

"Don't you?" Charles offered his arm, as if they were walking down the Charleston promenade. Millie took it, and they started up the road. "Who do you think rescued me from my life of leisure and ease, if not you? The first time I saw you at Roselands, sitting so straight at the piano, I thought I had stumbled upon—"

An Early Arrival

"Sitting at the piano?" Millie stopped him. "The first time you saw me was in Uncle Horace's study, and I had my teeth blacked out with wax."

"I don't remember that at all," Charles said. "I do remember that you were wearing a deep purple gown, and your hair was in golden ringlets. As I was saying, I thought I had discovered a princess being held captive by a wicked witch."

"That is not a nice way to refer to Aunt Isabel," Millie said, but she couldn't keep the giggle from her voice.

He lifted her over a puddle. "At any rate, I soon discovered that quite the opposite was true. I had stumbled upon a plot to overthrow the Evil Empire of the South, and the agent sent to spread dissent and cause commotion was more like an angel than a princess."

"Don't be ridiculous." It was dark enough now that she could not see his face, but she could hear the teasing in his voice.

"Not at all. Princesses never appear in church with mud behind their ears, or wander the streets of strange cities with runaway children in tow. Angels, on the other hand, are well known to be involved in such things as jail breaks, and get into all kinds of scrapes."

"Speaking of that," Millie said, stopping in the middle of the road, "I have something to talk to you about. Something so important that I just couldn't bring myself to spring it on you in a letter. Charles, I — "

"Miiii-llie!" She saw the light of a lantern at the same moment she heard her father's voice.

"We are over here, Pappa!" Millie called, and a lantern bobbed toward them.

"We?" Stuart held up the lantern. "Thank God you are safe. When Inspiration came home without you…Charles?"

Millie's Reluctant Sacrifice

"I was lost, but your daughter has been kind enough to show me the way," he said. "I would shake your hand, sir, but I have spent some time sitting in the mud...." Stuart was dumbfounded, so the rest of the way to Keith Hill was spent in explanations and glad greetings.

"I was so worried," Marcia said, wrapping a blanket around Millie's shoulders when they returned to the house. "We didn't even know you had taken Inspiration!"

"I told them you wouldn't fall off a horse," Fan said. "I told them."

"How did you get mud all over you, Millie," Annis asked, "if you didn't fall down?" Millie knew that she was blushing fiercely, and there was not a single thing she could do about it.

"Rescues can be messy," Aunt Wealthy said sensibly. "Now run and set another place at the table, Annis, while Marcia and I prepare Charles's room."

CHAPTER

4

Moonlit Prayers

The prayer of a righteous man is powerful and effective.

JAMES 5:16

*M*illie wiggled her fingers to adjust the fit of her riding gloves, feeling very much as if she were the lead character in a stage play entitled, "The Sunday School Teacher's Romance." Her audience was never more than a giggle away. For three days, Annis, Jasmine, and Runhilda had dogged her steps day and night. She had not had one opportunity to talk with Charles uninterrupted. *If I do not get to speak to him alone soon, Lord, this may well become "The Sunday School Teacher's Revenge!"*

"Must you wear the rose silk, Millie?" Annis sighed. "I think the twilight blue would be so lovely."

"I could not bear it if she were any more lovely," Charles said, attempting to straighten his cravat.

"I don't see why we can't go to the party," Runhilda said.

"Because we weren't invited," Annis said sadly.

"And it will go on past your bedtimes." The Chetwoods' dinner party would be the first opportunity Millie had found to be alone with Charles since her father had hailed them on the road. "But I will tell you all about it."

"You are going to have to ride sidesaddle," Fan pointed out.

"Your sister rides sidesaddle very well," Charles said, still fumbling with the ends of his cravat.

"Maybe I should go with you," Annis said, "and stay outside with the horses."

"Now, Annis," Fan said, "you know it isn't proper to go to parties to which you are not invited. How would the Chetwoods feel, with you plastered up against the window like a moth? It would ruin their appetites."

Millie's Reluctant Sacrifice

"Millie, you are a vision!" Aunt Wealthy said, coming into the parlor at that moment. "And you look lovely as well, Charles."

"I believe handsome was the desired effect," Charles said, giving his reflection a hopeless look. One end of his cravat drooped, and the other could only be described as perky.

"Of course that is what I meant," Aunt Wealthy said, pulling his cravat knot out and starting over again without so much as an "If-I-may."

"I'm certainly glad to hear it," Charles said, lifting his chin so the tiny woman could work. "I would not want to be asked to dance by any of the young men of Pleasant Plains."

Wealthy had adopted Charles Landreth on first sight, and now treated him no differently than she would Cyril or Don, picking lint from his lapel or trying to smooth away his cowlick. With Marcia away attending a sick neighbor, she felt it her duty to inspect the young couple before they presented themselves in public.

"How did you have this tied?" she asked.

"I can't recall, and I certainly can't do it again." Charles grimaced. "I've never mastered these blasted things. In the South, I had servants who tied them, or Otis helped me. Otis was a whiz with cravats."

"Have you heard from him?" Millie took her cap from Jaz's head, and put it on her own.

"Only that he will be here for the wedding," replied Charles.

"These things can be tricky," Aunt Wealthy said, and for a moment Millie was unsure whether she was referring to weddings or men's neckwear. "But if a thing's worth doing, it's worth doing well. That's what I always say. A twist here and a tuck there—perfect!"

Charles turned to look at himself in the mirror, and his eyebrows went up a hair. The cravat was tied to perfection, in a snowy waterfall not seen, Millie was sure, since Thomas Jefferson graced the White House. Annis covered her mouth to hide her giggles, but Charles bowed slightly.

"Thank you, Miss Stanhope," he said. "I could never in a hundred years have achieved this effect."

"I don't need to remind you to have Millie in at an appropriate hour," Aunt Wealthy said. "Oh! That's my tea! And dinner is no doubt burning!" She gave Millie a kiss and followed the whistle away.

"And have Inspiration and Joe home early, too," Fan said, her arms folded. "Horses need lots of rest, and keep them out of the mud. It took me forever to curry Inspiration's tail the last time, Millie."

Stuart Keith came in the front door just in time to hear Fan's admonition. He put his hat on the rack and turned to ask, "On your way to the Chetwoods?"

"Pappa," Millie said, "Mrs. Trenton has the fever, and Mamma and Adah have taken a tureen of soup to the family. Aunt Wealthy is cooking dinner for you and the girls."

"I see." Stuart shook his head at Charles's cravat. "That may be the way the younger generation does things, Mr. Landreth," he said, "but Dr. Chetwood is quite conservative. Why don't you let me have a go at it?"

"Please," Charles spread his hands helplessly. "Be my guest."

"If something is worth doing, it's worth doing well," Stuart said, pulling the ends of the cravat. "It's worth doing right."

"I've heard that said, sir." Charles met Millie's eyes over her father's head and winked.

53

Millie's Reluctant Sacrifice

"Turn around," Stuart commanded. "If you watch in the mirror, I will show you how to do this. Hold your arms out to your sides." Charles held his arms out at shoulder level like a stiff-winged bird, and Stuart reached around him. "Pretend these are your hands." He wiggled his fingers. "Now, you take the left end, and loop it thus…" He looped, tucked, and tied, leaning to one side so that he could see what he was doing in the mirror. "There." The neat, conservative knot did seem to suit the occasion. "Now about getting my daughter home on time —"

"Pappa!" Millie said. "Dr. Chetwood is very punctual and believes that everyone should get at least eight hours of sleep a night. I'm sure his dinner will be over by ten. And don't worry, Fan, dear; the horses will be kept in a nice, dry stable the whole time."

Millie and Charles were late leaving the house, and likely to be late to the dinner as well, a trait Mrs. Chetwood found most irritating. She was as exacting in her entertaining as Dr. Chetwood was about the business of his medical practice. Millie resisted the urge to kick Inspiration into a gallop until they were out of sight of the three forlorn little faces on the porch, but as soon as she had turned the corner, she could resist no more.

"You handle a horse very well, Mr. Landreth," she said, when they pulled up in the Chetwoods' drive at last.

"Of course," Charles laughed. "I was raised a southern gentleman. And if you think I ride well, you should see me dance!"

"I have seen you dance, sir."

"That's right, you have. And you have not danced with me nearly often enough. Now that we are engaged, I believe I shall take you dancing every night until the wedding."

"That will take a miracle in Pleasant Plains," Millie said with a laugh. "But I am certainly willing." She tossed her reins to the footman.

Charles caught her as she slid from the saddle, and swung her around before he set her on the ground. "How does my cravat look?"

"Well…" Millie reached for the ends.

"Have mercy!" Charles laughed, backing away. "My last recourse is to wear it with confidence—and trust I will set a new style."

Millie took his arm, and they walked toward the wide front steps together. Suddenly, Millie stopped and grabbed his arm. "Charles!"

"What is it?" Charles said, looking around in alarm.

"We are alone. For the first time in three whole days. And I have promised myself to discuss something very important with you the moment we were alone. Charles, I—"

"Ahem." The Chetwoods' stern-faced butler stepped from the shadows on the porch. "I must tell you, madam, that your confession of passion will not go unheard."

"I wasn't going to confess my passion," Millie said.

Charles looked at her and she felt the blush creeping up her face. "I wanted to discuss…China."

"China? My mother had a lovely pattern!" Charles leaned close to her ear. "I don't think he will believe that your mind was on dishes," and then more loudly for the butler's ears, he said, "You may have any kind of dinner-ware you wish." He drew her up the steps. "But just at this moment, I think we are late."

"Yes, sir." The butler took Millie's coat, bonnet, and gloves, then showed them into the music room. They were greeted by their hosts, as well as Zillah and Wallace Ormsby, Claudina and York Monocker, Helen and Joseph Grange, and Lu and Will Chetwood.

"Millie," Lu said, after they had been greeted. "I cannot imagine how you could properly plan a wedding in four months. It took me a year to plan mine. What were you thinking?"

"She was thinking that now that she has him, she does not want him to escape," Mrs. Chetwood said with a smile.

"I'm afraid there is no escaping from Millie." Charles heaved an exaggerated sigh. "If I went to the ends of the earth, I would be haunted by dreams of her."

"If I could persuade you to accompany me to the ends of the room, for a moment," Dr. Chetwood said, "I have something I would like to discuss with you."

"Tsk," Mrs. Chetwood said. "You must study your tactics, dear. You are defeated in this before you begin. You haven't the charm to convince him to leave her side. Besides, you won't have time to finish your discussion before the meal begins."

Mrs. Chetwood was interrupted by the sound of the silver bell summoning them to dinner. Charles offered Millie his arm, and they went into the dining room. A course of French onion soup was followed by roast venison, fried quail with cream gravy, sage dressing, creamed onions, cranberry salad, sauerkraut relish, baking powder biscuits, and cheese and apple pie. The food was excellent and varied, but the conversation was not, as Dr. Chetwood had strictly observed rules of conversation at his table. No hint of religion, politics, or popular novels was allowed, leaving very little, in Millie's opinion, to talk about. The young ladies questioned Charles about the parties in the South—the gowns, the music, and the dancing—while Mr. Grange appeared to doze over his soup, and Dr. Chetwood glanced from time to time at his gold pocket watch, as if he were late for an appointment.

"I'm sure this is simple compared to what you were used to," Helen said to Charles over a bite of cheese and apple pie. "But good cooks are hard to find."

"Everything was delicious." Charles inclined his head to Mrs. Chetwood. "My compliments to the hostess and to the cook."

The butler appeared and spoke close to Dr. Chetwood's ear. "Pardon me," the doctor said as he stood. "There has been an accident. It isn't serious, but I must go."

Charles rose as well. "If you don't mind, sir? Oof—" Millie's boot had connected with his shin a bit harder than she had intended. "And if Millie could accompany us?"

She stood before Mrs. Chetwood or the doctor could object, and followed Charles as he followed Dr. Chetwood, practically running to keep up with the men's longer strides once they left the dining hall.

An ashen-faced man in rough clothing was standing in the doctor's office. "Beggin' your pardon, sirs, ma'am." He pulled his cap off. "I wouldn't have bothered you in the evening an' all, but the missus insisted."

"What's the problem, man?" Dr. Chetwood snapped.

The man pulled up his trouser leg to reveal a bloody bandage. "Ax head came off while I was choppin' wood. Just sharpened 'er, too." He shook his head. "Won't stop oozin' and the missus sent me over. It was a gusher, sir."

"Well, let's see the damage." Dr. Chetwood shifted into his professional mode. To human beings he could be gruff and arrogant, but a patient was a different sort of thing, a puzzle to be analyzed, a machine to be repaired. Each injured limb, no matter whether it belonged to a rich man or a poor man, received the same meticulous treatment.

Charles pulled up a chair for the man and Dr. Chetwood cut the crude bandage away. Millie winced. The wound was deep, white shin bone showing where the flesh was separated.

"The missus was right," Dr. Chetwood said. "You need stitches if you are to mend properly. Would you like a glass of whisky before we begin?"

"I would," the man said, twisting his cap in his hands and swallowing hard. Millie took the bottle from the cabinet and poured a generous helping. The man downed it in one gulp and held the glass out for more.

"I don't think that will be necessary," Dr. Chetwood said dryly. "We want you to be able to find your way home. Blast!" He had the catgut and needle in hand and was turning the needle back and forth in the lamplight, trying to see the eye. He turned up the oil lamp and adjusted his spectacles. "Why must people insist on being injured at night? Does nature not provide enough daylight hours for mauling oneself?"

"It was daylight when I was choppin' the wood," the man said defensively. "Sun went down after."

"Will you allow me, sir?" asked Charles.

Dr. Chetwood handed Charles the needle and catgut, and he threaded the needle.

"Owww!" The patient pulled his leg away as soon as Charles touched it. "Jest give me a minute here," he said. "Jest a minute!"

"There, now," Millie said, taking his hand. "Tell me about your family. Do you have children?"

"Boy," he admitted. "A good 'un, too. His name's Tom."

"And Tom is brave, isn't he?"

"Brave as they come," the workman said, gripping Millie's hand harder as Charles started to work, making quick, neat stitches, pausing only to wipe away the blood when he couldn't see the edges of the wound.

Millie tried to focus on the man, rather than on what Charles was doing, asking questions about his family each time he stopped talking. Dr. Chetwood, however, adjusted his spectacles again, and leaned over to watch the work.

"Hmm," he grunted when the neat line of stitches was complete. "Not bad. Not bad at all."

"That's right good to hear," the poor patient said. "Now, if'n you'd let go of me, young lady, I'd be obliged. The missus wouldn't care to know I had been holding hands with another."

"Oh! I beg your pardon," Millie said, dropping his hand.

Both Dr. Chetwood and Charles looked pleased when the seeping blood did not appear.

"Would you join me for a cigar and a brandy?" Dr. Chetwood asked Charles after the patient had gone.

"A cup of coffee, if you have it," Charles said. "And I believe Millie could use a cup of tea."

"Ah! Pardon me! I had quite forgotten her. I'm not used to having females in my office. I think we will find what we need in the kitchen. I don't require the servants to stay up for me," he explained. "And I insist that the family does not. It could ruin their health. If you are marrying a doctor, my dear, you must get used to late nights and long days. Mrs. Chetwood will have gone to sleep by now."

They followed him down the quiet hall to the dark kitchen. The fire was still burning in the wood stove, the servants having cooked their own supper after the family had dined. The kettle was on the back of the stove and the water was hot, but no coffee could be found, so Charles had to settle for tea.

"You are marrying into one of the most respected, if eccentric, families in Pleasant Plains, young man. Now, Millie, let me have my say," he said as Millie pressed her lips together. *We are not eccentric in the least!* she objected to herself. "I am glad to see that you are bringing some scientific knowledge with you," the doctor continued. "This town and this country need it. I cannot deny the fact that I am getting on in years. I had great hopes that young Rupert Keith would join me in my practice. But he is pursuing a career as a pharmacologist."

"And quite gifted at it, I am told," Charles said with a smile.

"No doubt, no doubt. It takes every intelligence of man to fight disease. Well, enough beating around the bush. Pleasant Plains has grown beyond my ability to doctor. In short, young man, I would like you to consider not hanging out your own shingle just yet, but joining me in my practice. I feel no small responsibility to the people of this town. I want them to have the best. It would give me a chance to see your skill, sir. It would offer you the opportunity to have the most modern equipment available," he waved his hand at his office, "without the expense of setting it up. I stay on top of every scientific advance in medicine. And…if I am satisfied with you, when I die, this will be yours."

Charles put down his glass carefully. "That is a very generous offer, sir," he said.

"Nonsense. It is simple logic. Nature dictates that I will not be here forever, and the people of Pleasant Plains will need a doctor."

"Still, it is very kind. Millie and I will discuss the matter."

"Ah!" the doctor said. "One of those progressive types who discuss things with the wife!"

"I believe that is the way to marital harmony," Charles said.

"Nonsense," Dr. Chetwood waved the idea away as if it were a fly. "It is a scientific fact that the female's brain is smaller than the male's. They are designed to care for children, not make weighty decisions."

"Designed by whom?" Millie asked, making her eyes wide. She had been left out of this conversation long enough. "Doesn't a design imply a designer?"

"Nature itself," the doctor said, "dictates that a woman's role is to stay in the home, caring for the young."

"Have you considered the African lion?" Millie asked. "The female does all of the hunting, I understand. The males cannot take care of themselves!"

"Ah! A suffragette as well as an abolitionist! I should have known," Dr. Chetwood said, winking at Charles.

"The two go hand in hand, do they not? Why should a woman not vote?"

"Their brains are simply not adequate for it," the doctor said. "It has been my experience that women are better suited for domestic responsibilities. They do, however, make excellent nurses. The care and nurture of an invalid is best left to a woman's hand."

"My word!" Charles said. "Look at the time! I promised to have Millie home at a reasonable hour."

"Of course, you will take the surrey," Dr. Chetwood said. "She might fall off a horse."

"I will not fall off the horse," Millie said. "And I will not ride in the surrey."

Millie's Reluctant Sacrifice

"Suit yourself, then," Dr. Chetwood said, giving Charles a look that said, "See where this progressive thinking will lead?"

"Dr. Chetwood can be so…so aggravating," Millie said as they started home. "I was speechless."

"Hardly that," Charles replied. "It would take more than a mere doctor of modern science to render you speechless, my dear."

"I think I could be a doctor," said Millie.

"I think you should be my wife, and leave the doctoring business to me. Have you noticed, by the way?"

"Noticed?"

"That we are alone at last, riding slowly down a country lane under a bright moon. Didn't you have something…of importance…to discuss with me?"

"I do," Millie said. "When I mentioned China, I wasn't speaking of dinnerware. I meant the country of China." *It doesn't seem the right time to speak of it, but I can hardly turn back now.* "I believe you and I are called to the mission field in China," Millie blurted out.

There was a long moment of silence, and Millie wished that she could read his expression. When he still said nothing, Millie went on, describing the meeting where she had heard the voice of the Lord and the call to foreign missions.

"I am certainly willing to pray about it," Charles said at last. "I have never considered foreign missions, but I have learned that I can trust God to show me His will. If we are to be married, we must trust Him together, and trust each other as well." He stopped his horse.

"What are you doing?" Millie asked.

"I'm going to pray, of course," he said, climbing out of the saddle. He tied the reins to a branch, and then lifted

Moonlit Prayers

Millie down as well. He took her hand and led her to the middle of the road. He took off his jacket and spread it on the ground so that Millie would not spoil her dress, and they knelt together.

"Lord," Charles prayed, "I have given You my life, to spend as You choose, and Millie has given You hers as well. We are asking for Your will to be done in our lives, Lord. Show us where You want us to be."

They waited quietly, heads bowed, as the night sighed and rustled around them. Charles got to his feet at last and pulled Millie up as well, then lifted her to her saddle.

"Did you hear anything?" Millie asked.

"Only my heartbeat. It said...I love you."

Stuart and Marcia were waiting up for them, and Stuart and Charles put the horses in the barn while Marcia gave Millie the details of Mrs. Trenton's recovery.

After they had said good night, Millie went to her room and fumbled in the shadows for her prayer journal. She intended to write in the bright patch of moonlight on her bed, but she curled up hugging it to her chest instead.

What would I write? That God has not spoken to Charles about China? But didn't the Lord tell Mary about Jesus first, and then Joseph? Charles is a man of God, a man of prayer. Of course God will speak to him. The Scripture Millie wrote on the first page of every new prayer journal came to her: *Trust in the Lord with all your heart and lean not on your own understanding, in all your ways acknowledge Him, and He will make your paths straight.*

CHAPTER

Puddles of Heaven

In the last days, God says, I will pour out my Spirit on all people. Your sons and daughters will prophesy, your young men will see visions, your old men will dream dreams.

ACTS 2:17

Puddles of Heaven

*R*u, coming by boat, was the first of the Keith boys to arrive home for the wedding. Cyril and Don followed two days later by overland stage. Millie was surprised by the change in the twins. Their voices were deeper, booming through the halls and filling the rooms with laughter. Their red hair had darkened as well, and their shoulders were wider than Ru's, though they were still plagued with freckles. Marcia fussed over Cyril's hair, which was too long to suit her, and Aunt Wealthy fussed over their trousers, which had grown too short.

"And what is this?" Aunt Wealthy asked, leaning close and studying Cyril's upper lip.

"It's a moustache," Don answered for his twin. "At least it's trying to be. Good ol' Cy's hoping you will have some hair tonic that will make it more visible."

"A bit of shoeblack might help," Stuart suggested.

"Absolutely not!" Marcia said. "It would ruin my napkins!"

"It would be the wrong color anyway," Cyril sighed. "I guess I'm just going to have to keep working at this the old-fashioned way—prayer and perseverance."

Trunks were hauled to rooms, and it was as if Keith Hill had been sleeping and suddenly awakened. The bustling and activity of a full house brought new life back to Keith Hill.

"Millie!" Cyril caught her in the hall, the morning after his arrival. "I have something for you. I tried to find it last night, but it was at the bottom of my trunk. Wait right here!" He bounded up the stairs, his long legs taking them two at a time, and thundered down again with a book in his hands. "Here," he said, shoving it at her. "I was passing the bookshop, and it cried out to me from the window."

Millie turned it over. *A Pictorial Study of the Peoples of the World*, she read. She opened to the inscription, but Cyril clapped his hand over it.

"No! Don't read that yet! It's really a wedding present, you see, and that part's for both of you. I just could not wait to give it to you."

Millie turned to the middle of the book instead. Each page held a marvelous etching of a person in exotic dress, and a brief description of the subject. She looked up to find Cyril watching her eagerly.

"It means something, doesn't it?" he said. "I mean, there's a reason for it. I'm sure there is. I didn't hear a voice or anything, but when I looked at it, I knew I had to buy it." He leaned closer as if he were about to tell her a secret. "I think it was the Holy Spirit, Millie, telling me to buy it for you."

Millie couldn't help but smile. At that moment she had turned to a picture of a Chinese man. "It *was* the Holy Spirit, Cy."

"I knew it!" He smacked his fist into his palm. "I have been trying. Oh, not to be good—I tried that for years and never managed it. I've given that up…"

"Cy!" gasped Millie.

"It's not what you think. I've given up trying to be good, and now I just try to be with Jesus, and know He is with me. I try to talk to Him all of the time, like you do, Millie. And it's the strangest thing. I do right without thinking about it. It's like I'm Cyril of God, and…" His nose went up like a hound pup's, and Millie could have sworn his nostrils twitched. "What's that smell? Mamma's cooking pancakes!" He bounded down the hall, leaving Millie to shake her head. *Cyril of God. Who would have ever thought it? Thank You, Jesus,* she prayed.

"I will bring your children from the east and gather you from the west," Stuart quoted from the book of Isaiah when they were all seated at the breakfast table. "I will say to the north, 'Give them up!' and to the south, 'Do not hold them back.' Bring my sons from afar and my daughters from the ends of the earth." Millie was sure she had not seen such a twinkle in her father's eyes in months.

Marcia and Wealthy were happily cooking for everyone. Stuart never tired of listening to his tall sons' stories. Ru got up before dawn each morning to walk through his beloved garden or visit the sheds, a hammer in his hand and nails in his pockets.

Charles and Millie were relieved of their constant chaperones when Jaz convinced the girls that Cyril and Don were much more interesting to follow. The couple spent time walking and talking and praying together. *Charles still has not heard from the Lord.*

"I do have some concerns," he confessed, "as to whether I am fit for the mission field. I never knew what it was to need anything when I was growing up, and have hardly lived the life of a pauper in Chicago. Dr. Fox treated me as his own son."

"But when you were here the winter of the big snow, you carried packs of food to snowbound families while wolves tracked you!"

"I haven't forgotten a minute of it," Charles assured her. "Are there wolves in China?"

"Large bear-like creatures, I understand," Millie said. "They're called pandas, but they only eat bamboo. Are you sure you haven't heard from the Lord yet?"

Millie's Reluctant Sacrifice

"No letters at least. Tell me about your call again." So Millie told the story again of how the Holy Spirit had spoken to her during the missionary's talk.

Charles just shook his head. "I suppose we will just have to wait until God makes Himself more clear."

"I don't see how it could possibly be more clear," Millie said.

"Well, if God is calling us to China, how are we going to get there? I haven't the money set aside, and I assume that you don't either. And once we are in China, how will we live?"

"I haven't figured that out yet," Millie had to admit. "But Aunt Wealthy always says that when it's God's will, He makes a way. I'm sure they need doctors in China."

"I'm sure they do," Charles agreed. "That leaves us only the problem of getting there, and finding out who *they* are."

"You, sir, are too practical."

"Nonsense," Charles said. "You are the practical one. After all, you fell in love with me. And I, as you can see, fell madly in love with —"

Millie hit him playfully.

"Seriously, though," Charles said. "I have been talking to God about it, and these are questions I feel I need to have answered. I told your father I would take care of you. It's a husband's duty. God knows how I feel about this, and I am sure He can answer my prayers."

Millie took his arm, and they walked on in silence. *I'm sure You can, Lord*, she prayed. *And can You please hurry? It's hard being excited about this all by myself!*

With the house so full, Charles and Millie walked and talked outside at least two hours a day, but no one seemed to notice they were gone. Millie even found time to slip away to walk and talk with Jesus while Charles spent time with Stuart or the boys.

She was returning from one such talk when she found a young man on the doorstep dressed in a minister's coat and collar. A small boy stood beside him.

"Frank! Frank Osborne!" Millie took his hands. "How good to see you!"

There were grey streaks at Frank's temples, but his smile was warm. The boy looked up and Millie caught her breath, her heart hurting all at once. He had Annabeth's eyes!

"How do you do," Millie said, offering her hand. "My name is Millie Keith, and your mother was a very dear friend of mine."

"I am a little tired," the boy said seriously. "My name is Frank Too, and I don't 'member her."

"Well, Frank, I—"

"Frank Too," the boy corrected her. Then losing his courage, he hid behind his father's leg.

Frank spread his hands as if to say, "What's to be done?" Millie smiled.

"Very well then, Frank Too, I shall tell you all about her, all you want to know. We had marvelous adventures in Lansdale when we were both little girls."

There was no answer, and Frank just shook his head. Millie had always believed Frank to be capable of any task given him, but this one—to be a widower at such an early age, and with a small son to care for as well—seemed too much.

"How are you, Frank?" she asked.

"I don't quite know how to answer," Frank said. "The Millie I knew would see straight through a lie, and the truth is hardly something I would bring to a wedding. I might not

be here at all if your Aunt Wealthy hadn't insisted. But I am glad for your gladness, Millie."

"Well, come inside and make my family glad as well. I can't tell you how much it means to see a face from Lansdale!" She opened the door and ushered them inside, almost running into Adah in the entryway.

"Adah!" Millie caught her sister's elbow. "Look who's here!"

Adah looked over the stack of books she was carrying with an expression of expectation, but no light dawned on her face.

"It's Frank Osborne, from Lansdale! And this is his son, Frank Too."

"Oh!" Adah extended the hand that was not occupied with the books. "Mr. Osborne, I do remember you. You've grown shorter."

"I think perhaps it's you who has grown taller," Frank said. "I believe you were six when we last met."

"Eight," Adah corrected. "I was eight when we left Lansdale. I thought you were quite grown up, like all of Millie's friends."

"That was a long time ago." Frank almost managed a smile. "May I help you with those books?"

"No need," Adah said. "I was just returning them to the library. So nice meeting you again, and we are all so glad you could come."

"Books tend to wander up to Adah's room," Millie explained as Adah staggered away, "attracted by the quiet there. But every few weeks she must bring them out, or she would not be able to find her bed."

Frank was warmly welcomed by all and settled into Ru's room. A cot was added for Frank Too. That evening, when

Stuart asked Frank to lead the family in Bible reading, he turned to Psalm 100. "Shout for joy to the Lord, all the earth…"

Millie was sure he had chosen the psalm as a blessing for her family, and not a reflection of his own heart. When she bowed her head to pray, it was Jeremiah 8:21 that came to mind: *Since my people are crushed, I am crushed; I mourn, and horror grips me. Is there no balm in Gilead? Is there no physician there? Why then is there no healing for the wound of my people?*

You are the only physician that can heal his hurts, Lord, Millie prayed silently. *Heal his grieving heart.*

After some hymns were sung, Marcia, Wealthy, and Millie applied themselves to the last of the sewing, while Stuart, Charles, and Frank talked on the couch. Frank Too curled up in Ru's lap, watching the twins play chess. But Adah sat listening to her father and Frank, her book forgotten on her lap.

"You were having quite an intense conversation," Millie said, settling on the couch with Stuart and Charles after Frank left to put his son to bed.

"Frank Osborne has an amazing faith for one so young," Stuart said. "He has lost his mother and his wife, and yet there is no bitterness in him. Only a trust of his Savior."

"And sadness," Adah said.

"Yes, and sadness," Stuart agreed.

~~~~~

Frank settled in at Keith Hill, clearly enjoying the good spirits around him but unable to shine himself. Millie was sure that God had brought him there when she saw his slow smile, heard him joking with the boys, or saw him walking through the garden talking earnestly with Stuart.

Millie's Reluctant Sacrifice

The joy at Keith Hill was contagious, spilling over the next Sunday at church. As a result, the Ormsbys, Lightcaps, and Lords were invited to an impromptu picnic on the wide, cool riverbank beneath Keith Hill. They went to their own homes only long enough to gather baskets of food, and for the children to change out of their Sunday best. Jasmine arrived in new swimming attire, with crisp red and white stripes, and Annis begged to change into her suit as well so that they could wade or catch crayfish under the grassy banks. Marcia agreed, provided Millie would check on them now and then to make sure they were not wading too deep.

Wealthy and Marcia sliced cold ham and made biscuits and hard-boiled eggs. Ru found a watermelon that had volunteered to grow in his old garden, and by way of a net, lowered it into the well to chill. Stuart made sure the dock and the rowboat were shipshape, and by mid-afternoon the picnickers were strolling, rowing, or just enjoying conversation in the shade of the huge trees.

Reverend Matthew Lord was naturally drawn into conversation with Frank and Charles. The two young ministers had much in common. Millie listened as Matthew started expanding the points he had made in his sermon, the text of which had been Luke 11:2, that portion of the Lord's Prayer in which Jesus taught His disciples to ask for the Kingdom to come.

"I wouldn't suggest returning to a monarchy," Frank said. "But I do think that we as Americans have lost an understanding of the Kingdom of God, because we have no king."

Millie leaned over in order to see the girls more clearly. They were wading in the shallow water by the shore.

Puddles of Heaven

"If His will were done, would earth be like Heaven?" Charles asked. The sound of Charles's voice brought Millie's attention back to the conversation. He had been very quiet, even after church, as if there were something on his mind.

"I believe little bits of it already are," Frank said. "Wealthy Stanhope's house has been a sanctuary for me these last few years," he said. "It is as if Heaven has leaked, and a puddle of it exists in her home. God has wiped the tears from my eyes there, though he has used Wealthy Stanhope's handkerchiefs to do it. Keith Hill seems to be like that as well—a city of refuge in a broken world."

"I wish we had a whole town full of houses such as that," Matthew Lord said. "Stuart and Marcia have taught me a great deal about living my faith."

"My greatest difficulty," Frank said, "is motivating people to live the Word of God, and not to hear it only."

"If you gentlemen will excuse me," Millie said, "I promised Mamma I would watch the children." Millie took Charles's hand and they walked together along the grassy shore, stopping to watch a great battle among the tree roots. Matthew Boone had brought a pocketful of lead soldiers, and he was playing the part of the patriots, while Frank Too led the ill-fated redcoat band.

Fan had taken the girls to the pier, and they were dangling their toes in the water. Joy Everlasting's red head was bent toward Runhilda's blonde one, but Jaz's wild curls were missing.

"Do you see Jasmine anywhere?" Millie asked. Charles shook his head. "I thought she was at the pier with the others."

"She went that way," Fan said, pointing down the path beside the riverbank. "She was angry, but I told her not to go too far. Listen, you can hear her." It wasn't Jasmine that they heard, but a splash.

"She's throwing rocks," Annis explained. "She always does that when she is mad."

"Did someone say or do something unkind to her?" Millie asked.

Runhilda shook her head. "We didn't," she said pointedly.

"Yeah," Joy Everlasting echoed. "We didn't."

"I see," Charles said. "Would you care to continue our stroll, Miss Keith?" They walked hand in hand down the path until they found Jasmine and the small mountain of rocks she had gathered. The little girl squinted at the afternoon sparkles on the river, then sent a rock skipping across them.

"Is something wrong?" Millie asked, as Jaz picked up another rock.

"Cyril," Jaz said as she sent the rock spinning after the previous one, "said—" She threw another, and then turned to Millie. "He said I...I looked like a peppermint stick!"

"Well," Millie said, trying to keep the smile from her face, "peppermint is...um..."

"Is what?" Jaz demanded, picking up another rock.

"Peppermint is very sweet," Charles offered.

"I don't want to be sweet!" She flung the rock with all her might, not even bothering to skip it. "And I don't want to be a stick. I just want to be alone."

Charles looked at Millie, and she shook her head. "I like to be alone too sometimes," she said. "Charles and I are just going to sit on that log over there."

Millie sat on the log, where she could keep an eye on all of the girls at once.

Puddles of Heaven

"What do you think?" Charles asked, sitting down beside her. Jaz was working her way through the pile of rocks.

Millie looked across the water to where Cyril pulled the oars of the rowboat, while Emmaretta Lightcap twirled her lace parasol and laughed. "I think my brother had better stay well out of throwing range."

"Oh, I understand," he nodded. "I believe you are right, Miss Keith."

"You seem very pensive today," Millie said. "You've hardly said ten words since church."

"Do you believe that God still speaks to people in dreams?"

"I don't see why He shouldn't," Millie said. "Though He has never spoken to me in one. Why do you ask?"

"I had a dream last night. A very young man standing with his hands outstretched to me said, 'Come and help us.' "

A thrill shot through Millie. "Just like the story in the Bible!" she exclaimed.

"When the man from Macedonia called out to Paul," Charles nodded. "It was very like it. So much so that I'm not sure I wasn't just dreaming the Scripture because I had read it recently." He shook his head. "It seemed so real. He was wearing odd clothes and a strange hat...and he wasn't speaking English, come to think of it. But I knew what he was saying anyway. 'Come and help us.' He said it twice."

"Keep an eye on the girls, just for a moment!" Millie said. She hurried up the hill, almost missing her footing on the steps in her eagerness to get into the house and to her room. She pulled Cy's book from the shelf and ran back down the terraced steps to the riverfront. She sat beside Charles on the log and flipped to the picture of the Chinese peasants.

Millie's Reluctant Sacrifice

"Here!" She held it up triumphantly. "This is what he looked like, isn't it?"

Charles studied the picture for a long moment. Finally, he lifted his eyes. "No."

"No? Look at the hat!" Millie insisted. "He's wearing a funny hat."

"I am looking," Charles said. "That's not it. His clothes were different, more colorful. And the hat was," he sketched a box in the air, "… flat."

"Ohhhh," Millie groaned, closing the book. "It was just an ordinary dream."

Charles took the book from her lap and started to flip the pages idly. "I suppose it was. As I said, I had just read that story —" Suddenly he stopped. "The man looked more like this. In fact…" He held the book up so that he could see the etching more clearly. "This is exactly what he was wearing."

Millie looked over his shoulder. The man in the picture was wearing baggy pants and something that resembled a blanket. He did indeed have a square hat on his head. "A Quechua Indian of Bolivia," she read. "Bolivia is nowhere near China. Did you have sausages for supper last night?"

"Come to think of it, I did." Charles had a wrinkle between his brows. "But I have eaten sausages all my life, and they have never caused me to dream of South American Indians before. Certainly not a South American Indian begging for my help. This is a collection of etchings." He looked at the cover to make sure. "Perhaps I have seen the picture somewhere before."

"Perhaps you —" Millie began, but was interrupted by a scream. She leaped from the log and was running before the first sound faded away, with Charles right behind her. They joined the crowd that had formed around Matthew Boone.

Puddles of Heaven

His mother soon discovered that the little boy had stepped on a bee. She removed the stinger from his little bare foot while Matthew Boone sobbed into her apron. The paste of baking soda and tobacco juice that Aunt Wealthy put on the sting did not seem to help, but the coonskin cap that Don found in his closet miraculously dried up the tears, and turned the injury into the honorable wound of a mountain man. And when Cyril asked Jasmine to hold Matthew Boone on her lap so he could take them out in the boat, it was salve for two wounds.

The picnickers did not leave until the fireflies began to rise from the grass. Then one by one they said their good-byes and started home, the littlest ones sleeping in their mothers' arms or on their fathers' shoulders.

Perhaps Frank is right, Lord, Millie prayed as they waved good-bye. *Perhaps a little bit of Heaven has leaked onto Keith Hill — a little puddle of Your Kingdom. That's what I want my home with Charles to be. That's what I want to take with us to China — Your Kingdom. Speak to Charles soon, Lord! He is listening so hard!*

6

Fish, Fowl, or Human

*But blessed is the man who trusts
in the Lord, whose confidence is
in him. He will be like a tree
planted by water that sends
out its roots by
the stream.*

JEREMIAH 17:7–8

Fish, Fowl, or Human

With a little over a week until the wedding, the dresses were done, the cake baked and ready to be iced, the decorations prepared, and small gifts made and wrapped for the members of the wedding party.

"The only things missing," Millie said, "are the best man and a revelation for Charles!"

Celestia Ann looked up from the notes Charles and Millie had written about their vows. "I think the ceremony will be wonderful, and the marriage as well, even if the revelation does not arrive. Ru could stand in Otis's place, couldn't he? Has Effie agreed to play the piano?"

"She has," Millie said. "Ru may be able to stand in Otis's place at the ceremony, but he will not be able to make arrangements for the honeymoon."

"That is the best man's job, isn't it?" Celestia Ann tapped her lips with her finger. "Perhaps you should simply board a rowboat and start down the river."

"Don't tease," Millie said. "It's eight days until my wedding, my bags are packed, and I have no idea where we are going. Charles simply says not to worry, Otis said he would make the arrangements."

"He didn't tell Charles what arrangements he was going to make?"

"Apparently not. Not even a hint."

"I think it's a good beginning," Celestia Ann said, handing Millie the copy of her wedding vows. "Your marriage will start with mystery and adventure!" She picked up Mary Grace, who was leaning on her mother's leg. "Don't worry so much, Millie. All you really need is the groom, and the minister, of course. But I'll make sure he is at the church on time. Have you discussed children?"

"Number, but not names. Charles says that he believes twelve would be too many," Millie said. "I tend to agree."

"If you do have twelve, I would suggest one name a-piece. If you give them each two, you will run out too soon. Speaking of children," Celestia Ann's eyes danced, "here comes Gavriel Lightcap."

"You can't mean it!" Millie said, leaning over to watch Gavi stoop to kiss little Matthew Boone on her way to the door. He wiped the kiss off and made a face.

"Yes, I can," Celestia Ann said, as Gavi came in the door. "She hasn't told me yet, but I believe the next citizen of Pleasant Plains will be a Lightcap!"

"How could you possibly have known?" Gavi said. "I haven't even told Gordon yet!"

"Oh, I notice things," Celestia Ann said, "like a certain flush to your cheeks and a special smile when you were holding Mary Grace last Sunday."

"You do beat all," Gavi shook her head.

Two days later, there had still been no note or letter from Otis Lochneer. Millie could not help but mention it when she handed Charles the picnic basket she had packed.

"He will be here," Charles said with certainty. "Even if flood and fire should bar his way, Otis will be at my wedding."

"That wasn't my impression of him at all," Millie said.

"Otis has the heart of a lion," Charles whispered, "under the hide of a lamb." Millie raised one eyebrow. "He does,"

Charles insisted. "You simply need to know him better. You have only seen him at parties and in bad company."

"I was unaware that he had a life outside of parties and bad company." Millie was sorry as soon as she said it, for she saw the hurt in Charles's eyes. "I didn't mean that the way it sounded," she said. "It is true that I have only seen Otis at parties and in bad company. But I should have known by your friendship that there is more to him than I have seen."

"There is," Charles agreed. "God had an excellent man in mind when He created Otis Lochneer. Where are we going?" He held the garden gate open for her.

"Only to one of my favorite places on earth," Millie said. "The muskrat pond. I discovered it when I was a young girl, and I have had many daydreams there."

"Were any of them about me?"

"I'm afraid so," Millie laughed. "I told the muskrat all kinds of secrets about you."

"Then I shall have to meet this furry gentleman!"

Millie led him to the wooden bridge that crossed the creek, but here they left the beaten path. The game trails across the marsh changed from time to time, an old path being swallowed up by brush, a new one emerging. Millie found she could navigate by certain trees and stumps and find her way quite well, even if they occasionally had to duck under a branch, or turn sideways because the game trail was so narrow. Here and there Millie lifted her skirts and jumped from grass patch to grass patch, as the ground had become very soggy.

The wet summer had been good for the Kankakee. The pools were full and the streams ran clear. There were clouds of butterflies and the almost constant buzz of bees going about their work.

Millie's Reluctant Sacrifice

"Tell me about Otis," Millie said when they finally reached the tussock of grass above her pond. "Wait! There he is!" She grabbed Charles's arm and pointed. A muskrat was busy beneath them, his presence made known by a purposeful ripple on the pond's surface.

"I thought for a moment you meant Otis," Charles whispered as the furry brown face appeared. "I couldn't imagine what he was doing here."

Millie laughed out loud, and the muskrat disappeared with a *plosh!*

"I don't think your friend was too impressed with the secrets you told him about me. He doesn't seem to want to get acquainted."

"He may be jealous," Millie said. "But do tell me about Otis."

"Well," Charles said, as Millie spread the picnic blanket under the huge tree that shaded the pond, "he's very fond of sweets, excellent with cravats, and…he would lay down his life for a friend. You have no idea how much he has risked by staying loyal to me, Millie."

"Half of the mothers in the South would be delighted if their daughters married Otis!" Millie said.

"For his fortune, yes," Charles agreed. "And just as happily stab him in the back for his loyalties. Do you realize he challenged a man to a duel on my behalf?"

"I can't believe it!"

"But it's true. He was present when relations of the Breandans called me an abolitionist and a coward because I had left the South rather than face charges of slave stealing."

"I was the one who stole the slaves," Millie said. "You only helped."

"No doubt that Otis told them this," Charles said. "He informed the slanderer that although I was an abolitionist, I was no coward, and he would prove the point on my behalf."

"What happened?" Millie asked, trying to reconcile this warlike image with that of the plump, golden-haired young man she knew from the Dinsmores' parties.

"Otis was waiting at the appointed spot at dawn the next day with pistols. The Breandans' man did not show up." Charles shrugged.

"And Otis told you this?"

"Certainly not. I would not have known about it at all if word of it had not come to Mrs. Travilla. She wrote to me begging me to tell Otis not to do such a thing again. Millie," Charles took her hands, "Otis has his faults. I know that Otis talks too much. It was his fault that you were sent home, and that I had to leave the South. But I have forgiven him, and I hope you have as well."

"Of course, I have," Millie said, but her heart tugged as she said it.

"I would like you to pray for his salvation. He could use his talents for the Lord."

"And his shortcomings, as well," Millie said. "There's a place in the Kingdom for those who talk too much. They're called evangelists."

"Or martyrs," Charles suggested. "I'd rather he not be called that."

Charles started to unpack a feast of boiled eggs, watermelon rind, pickles, tarts, and summer sausage. Last, he pulled out the book Millie had put in the bottom of the basket. "*Missionaries to China*. Is this a little light reading for our picnic?"

Millie's Reluctant Sacrifice

"The stuff that dreams are made of," said Millie as she tucked a napkin demurely over her lap. "Sausages, sweet mustard, and books."

⁓

That night Millie opened her prayer journal to the long list of people she prayed for daily. There were stars by some of the names, like little Elsie Dinsmore's, showing that God had answered her prayers, and stars all around Charles's name, but Otis was not on the list. She had known that Otis was Charles's best friend, of course, but he had been an irritation to her. *If Charles's heart hurts for him, Jesus' heart must hurt even more.* Millie dipped her nib in the ink and added Otis's name to the end of the list. That night when she knelt by her bed, Otis Lochneer was the first person she prayed for.

On the evening of the fourth day before the wedding, Aunt Wealthy went to answer the door and returned with a plump little man in a blue topcoat, yellow cravat, and yellow pants. His tight curls peeked from under the hat he quickly removed, bowing to the ladies. Millie couldn't help but think that if the fat cherub babies from the paintings of Raphael ever grew up and lost their wings, they would look exactly like this.

"Otis!" Charles jumped across the room and shook his friend's hand. Then he turned to introduce him to the Keiths. A name alone, it seemed, could never explain Otis Lochneer—a chapter at least was needed. As Charles launched into the attempt, Annis leaned close to Millie. "He's dressed like a parrot," she whispered.

"Annis!" Millie mouthed back. "It's impolite to whisper."

"What if you don't want them to hear it?" Annis's voice was a little louder.

"Shush," Millie whispered, flushing as Charles glanced at them. "If you do not want them to hear, do not say it at all."

Otis clapped his hands at the stories Charles was telling, and jewels flashed from the half-dozen rings he wore. This seemed to fascinate Cyril and Don, who, from the looks on their faces, were still trying to figure out whether he was fish, fowl, or human being.

"You assisted in Luke and Laylie's escape, Mr. Nocklear?" Aunt Wealthy asked.

"Lochneer. I did not, not really. I merely turned my back at an opportune moment. I am afraid I must think of it as abetting in the banishment of my friend, and the gravest mistake I ever made. I have suffered greatly for it."

"Your mistake was not in turning your back when you did," Charles said. "It was in speaking of it at the wrong time. But it is forgiven." He slapped Otis's shoulder. "After all, if I had not lost all of my worldly fortune, I would not have found my Savior."

Otis rolled his eyes. "A reservation in the eternal is all well and good, but—" His pink hand smacked his forehead. "Charles, I left your great-grandfather on the porch!"

Marcia stood quickly, but Charles waved her back. "Great-grandfather won't mind," he said. "He has been dead for sixty years."

"Oh, dear," Aunt Wealthy said, but Don stood up.

"I'll let him in, then." He returned carrying what could only be a large portrait wrapped in oil paper and tied with string. Cyril cut the cords with his pocketknife, and Otis pulled the paper away.

Millie's Reluctant Sacrifice

"Oh, my," Aunt Wealthy said again, and that seemed to sum up the feelings of the entire Keith clan. Millie found herself staring into the disapproving eyes of a grim, grizzled old man. She moved to stand closer to Charles, but it didn't help. The portrait was so cunningly drawn she could not escape the gaze.

"Millie, you remember Grandfather John Quimbly Landreth?" Millie nodded. She dimly recalled seeing this portrait in a hall of dead ancestors at the Landreth mansion. The memory sent shivers down her spine. "But why?" Charles turned to Otis.

"Because you are the last of the Landreths," Otis said solemnly. "And everyone should have friends and family present when they wed. Your Aunt refused to come, though I offered to escort her."

Charles started to laugh. "John Q. always was my favorite," he said. "He contributed greatly to the family fortune, if not our honor."

"I knew he was the one you'd want!" Otis's rings flashed. "The rest of the dead relations are stored in a shed behind the Charity Home where your Aunt insists on residing. She won't part with them. If she is to live a life of frugality, then they must too. They sit in the dark with spiders." He shuddered. "And other unpleasant things."

"I'm surprised she allowed you to bring Great-grandfather," Charles said, stepping closer to the portrait. Millie was surprised to see a resemblance in the lift of the eyebrow and curve of the lip.

"Well, er, let me tell you the truth." Otis turned a lovely shade of shell pink. "She didn't know the old gent was coming along with me. Still doesn't know he's gone, I hope."

90

"Did he steal Charles's great-grandfather?" This time Annis's whisper was loud enough for everyone to hear.

"Of course not," Cyril said. "He only stole a painting of him."

Otis turned from pink to red. "I thought…at the time I felt it was the right thing to do. I plan to return him after the ceremony."

"The portraits are mine, really," Charles said, patting his friend's shoulder, though in Millie's mind this did not excuse the theft. Otis hadn't known it, after all. "And Grandfather would have approved of sneaking away. He was, after all, a privateer."

"Not really!" Cyril examined the portrait more closely. "Millie will be related to a pirate?" Don stepped closer to the painting as well.

Millie took the opportunity to pull Annis aside. "You mustn't whisper about people," she said. "It's rude."

"But you whispered back!"

"I had to or they would have heard me!"

"That's why I was whispering in the first place," Annis said. "How am I supposed to know not to whisper, if I can't ask?"

"That's a good question," Millie said. "How about this? From now on, if you should be quiet, I'll…I'll blink. Like this." Millie batted her eyelashes. "That means we will talk about it later, all right?" Annis batted her eyelashes back. "Good," Millie said, and turned to the conversation around the portrait.

"Nonsense," Charles was saying, in what Millie thought was a very good imitation of his aunt. "A patriot, practically a saint. He only plundered British ships."

Cyril was the first to warm to Otis. Don followed suit, and soon they were laughing at his tales of southern

Millie's Reluctant Sacrifice

chivalry. He was the hero of his own tales, and always well intentioned, but they never seemed to work out the way he had planned. And he seemed just as baffled as his audience when his story took a bizarre and hilarious twist, leaving him laughing at himself, and the Keiths laughing with him. The laughter went on until Marcia sent the younger children to bed.

"I'm sure Charles and Millie would like to talk with Otis alone," she said, and the others said their good nights as well, wishing them sweet dreams and God's blessings while they slept.

"You certainly have found a religious lot, Charles," Otis said. "Pardon me, Millie, but I do remember that you were quite extreme about these things, and I know now how you came by it." He settled into a comfortable chair. "I meant what I said about making it up to you, Charles. I have a granduncle, you know, Uncle Yancey Lochner"

"I hope you haven't left him on the porch also," Millie said.

"I hope not as well," Charles laughed. "I seem to recall he has a wicked way with a cane—at least for boys who stole his cigars."

"That's true," Otis said. "He also has a daughter who married a Spanish gent with mining interests in Bolivia."

CHAPTER 7

Wedding Vows and New Adventures

The Lord had said to Abram, "Leave
your country, your people and your
father's household and go to the
land I will show you."

GENESIS 12:1

A chill raced down Millie's spine as Charles turned toward his friend.

"Uncle Rael is expanding his mining operations," Otis went on, oblivious to Millie's worried look, "and I believe he has a position which might interest you."

"I'm not a mining engineer," Charles said.

"Of course not. Uncle Rael is building a clinic for the Indians who work in his mine. It makes the government look favorably on him, but that is not his only reason. Aunt Angela is not well. Their village is in a remote corner of the country and there are no doctors for miles. I told my uncle that I had the perfect man for the job."

Charles started pacing, his hands locked behind his back. Millie was shaking her head, but neither man seemed to notice.

"Ah!" Otis beamed. "I see I have your interest. I cannot restore your fortunes, Charles, but this can go a long way toward doing so. Uncle is offering a very generous salary. It could lead to speculation in the mine, possibly a partnership. My uncle is a very generous man."

"And?" Charles stopped pacing. "There is something you are not telling me."

"And I am going down to Bolivia myself. Father has invested a good sum in steam engines to pump water from the mines. He wants me to watch over his investment."

This time Charles shook his head, and Millie sighed with relief.

Otis put up a hand. "Now, don't say no before you have had time to think about it. The journey would be difficult, it's true, but Millie is used to the frontier life. Uncle Rael will pay for your travel, of course, and once you arrive at the Hacienda, you will live like a lady of quality should. It's practically a palace. It's an opportunity, I assure you."

Charles had a dazed look on his face. If Otis had been eavesdropping he could not have answered Charles's questions about travel more concisely. His eyes went to Millie, and she shook her head.

"I told you I would make it up to you," Otis said, standing as well. "Come and help us."

"What?"

"I said, come and help us," Otis repeated, looking a little befuddled himself. "I mean me, of course. Come and help me."

"We will need time to discuss it," Charles said, but Otis could hear the change in his voice as clearly as Millie could, and he was smiling.

They said good night to Otis, and before Millie could say a word, Charles caught her hands. "Did you hear that? God is calling us—to Bolivia!" he said. "I am as sure as I have ever been of anything in my life. 'Come and help us!'"

"But…don't you think you would have seen Otis's uncle calling you in a dream? Or Otis for that matter? We would be going to live in a palace—Otis said so himself. Missionaries don't live in palaces."

"They do if that's where God puts them," Charles said. "Didn't the apostle Paul say that he had learned to be content in much and in little? Paul made tents; I will be a doctor to miners and Spanish royalty. But my true job will be preaching Jesus to the Quechuas."

"But China…"

"Millie," Charles got down on his knees beside her. "You must know that I will not go without you. And if God does

Wedding Vows and New Adventures

not tell you the same thing, then I will be sure that I am wrong. But let me ask you some questions." Millie nodded at him. "Did God tell you to go to *China*? Or are you simply called to foreign missions?"

Millie blinked. *Tell them.* That's all God had said. "I need to pray about this," Millie said. "I need some time with Jesus."

That night, she paced the floor of her room, her Bible open on her desk and a book of maps on her bed. "I know nothing about Bolivia, Lord!" She knelt and prayed, then paced some more. "But Lord! You did tell me I was going to China, didn't You?" She picked up the book Cy had given her, intending to turn to the picture of China, but the book opened to the inscription page instead.

To Charles and Millie Landreth, .
I will give you the treasures of darkness, riches stored in secret places, so that you may know that I am the Lord, the God of Israel, who summons you by name.
Isaiah 45:3

May God bless your union, C. o. G.
(Cyril of God)

Charles and Millie Landreth. The bookplate in the front of every one of Millie's books on China read: *Miss Millie Keith.*

"You knew Charles was coming back, didn't You, Lord?" Millie said. "You are calling Mr. and Mrs. Landreth to serve You together—to serve You as one. That's why You only gave me part of the puzzle and gave the rest to Charles. I hope that's what it means, because I feel exactly as if I am jumping off a cliff!"

Millie pulled her books on China down from the shelf. She found an empty hatbox and put them in it, and then

97

quickly closed the lid. "Lord, I give China back to You." She slid the box under her bed, so far back her fingers could barely touch it. "I will trade it for Your secrets hidden in darkness and for Charles going with me to find them."

Her bookshelf looked very empty with only her Bible and prayer journal and the three volumes Aunt Wealthy had sent her. Had a book about Bolivia ever been written?

"Bolivia?" Stuart Keith dropped his fork and sat back in his chair. "I had considered your moving to Chicago, daughter, but Bolivia? You would be gone for years!"

The Keiths were looking at Millie and Charles in varying degrees of dismay. Don and Cyril sat on the edges of their seats, as if it were their own fates being decided. Aunt Wealthy had her chin down, and Millie was sure she was praying. Annis looked as if she were going to cry.

"It has been something of a surprise to me, Pappa," Millie admitted. "Though not completely so. I have felt for almost a year that I am called into the foreign mission field." Millie began to explain how God had prepared her heart and about her prayer with Charles on the road. Otis took over when she reached the part about his uncle's offer, painting the position in such glowing terms that it seemed too good to be true, but everyone at Keith Hill was quite accustomed to him by this time and only smiled and nodded.

"So you would be going in order to be a doctor," Stuart said.

"Not exactly, sir." Charles described his dream and finding the Quechua man in Millie's book. "I believe we are being called to Bolivia as missionaries. My medical practice is merely a tentmaking skill."

Stuart shook his head. "We have let Millie go twice now, once to Roselands and once to New Orleans, and I think that is quite enough. Have you considered Dr. Chetwood's offer? We do need another doctor here in Pleasant Plains."

Marcia stood and put her hand on her husband's shoulder. "We must let her go again, Stuart," she said. "I see the fingerprints of God all over it. Let her go, and trust that God will bring her home again, just as you said."

"I did?"

"Don't you remember the Scripture you prayed over them the first day the boys were home? 'Bring my sons from afar and my daughters from the ends of the earth.' God knew He was calling our Millie far away, even then."

Millie saw the tears in Stuart's eyes, and she thought that her heart would break, but he finally nodded, putting his hand over Marcia's as he spoke. "I agree. We will trust that God will bring you back to us. Both of you."

There was a moment of silence around the table as the family realized that Millie was really truly going, then Aunt Wealthy clapped her hands.

"How incredibly exciting!" she said. "Foreign missions is quite different, you know."

"Why?" Fan asked.

"I have given it a great deal of thought," Aunt Wealthy said. "I believe this is the reason: the Pilgrims and the Puritans who first came to this land were looking for a place to worship God, and that has become part of our culture. Even those poor souls who do not know Jesus are influenced by the huge number who do. Very few people here worship demons, or false gods."

Millie's Reluctant Sacrifice

"Demons? Surely you do not mean devils?" Otis said. "No one can say that the moral influence of religion is not beneficial to a society, Miss Stanhope. But believing in them is taking things a bit too far. They are just the product of a medieval mind."

"Are they?" Aunt Wealthy looked amused. "How then can one explain the words of the great missionary Paul: 'Finally, be strong in the Lord and in his mighty power. Put on the full armor of God so that you can take your stand against the devil's schemes. For our struggle is not against flesh and blood, but against the rulers, against the authorities, against the powers of this dark world and against the spiritual forces of evil in the heavenly realms'? In lands where demons are openly worshiped, things are quite different than they are here, I assure you. And those who go into missions are not staying in the safe community of believers. They are going to war." Wealthy's eyes flashed. "Not for land and borders, but for the eternal souls of men!"

Otis was looking quite alarmed, but Don leaned forward in his seat. "We were discussing this very thing in our campus Bible club," he said. "And one of the fellows said we should not even speak of such things, lest we attract their attention."

"Attract their attention? Pish-tosh," Wealthy said with a wave of her hand. "You don't imagine a missionary can march into a land that is bound in spiritual darkness and announce freedom for the captives without those spiritual powers of evil noticing? Of course they do, and they try to stop the preaching of Jesus with every wile at their disposal."

"That sounds quite frightening to me," Adah said.

"That's what the armor of God is for, my dear," said Aunt Wealthy, taking Adah's hand.

"Our Lord Jesus has won the victory for us," Millie said simply. "It may be war, but whether we live or whether we die, our future is secure in Jesus." She looked at Charles. "Our only concern is to follow Him the best we can."

"How soon would you leave?" Stuart asked.

Charles cleared his throat. "Immediately after the wedding. We would honeymoon in New York City, and then set sail. It would get us around Cape Horn at the best possible time."

"Yes, of course," Stuart said. "The weather is a consideration."

"But, Millie!" Fan said. "That's only four days away! You simply can't get married, pack up, and leave. You can't be going to some foreign land where anything could happen. Anything at all!"

The Keiths were quiet for the rest of the meal, and Marcia and Stuart the quietest of all. That evening, after the others had gone to bed, Millie found her parents sitting quietly in the parlor, holding hands before the fire. She could not think of one thing to say, so she sat at her mother's feet. Marcia brushed and braided her hair, just as she had done when Millie was a little girl.

The day of the wedding dawned with rainbows in the dewdrops. Millie had thought she would not sleep a wink, but here it was, past sunrise, and the delicious smell of the wedding breakfast was drifting up the stairs, along with the sounds of joy and laughter. Someone was singing—Ru, Millie decided, as the voice was too deep to be Stuart's— and Zillah was laughing.

Millie's Reluctant Sacrifice

Millie got out of bed, closed her curtains, then crawled back in and pulled the covers over her head.

"Courage!" Marcia said, pulling the covers down.

"How did you know?" Millie asked.

"I was married once myself," her mother laughed, "and I remember it very well."

"After today, I won't be Millie Keith anymore," Millie said, a little wistfully. "I have no question that I love Charles," Millie said. "But...what if I am not any good at being married?"

"You cannot practice being Charles's wife ahead of time," Marcia said. "All you can do is be the Millie Keith that God intended. And just as He saw each of you through every part of your life, He will be with you both in this marriage. Now let's get you into your dress. The boys are distracting Charles so that you can get away to the church without his seeing you—unless you have decided to leave him at the altar."

"Of course not!" Millie threw off her covers. "Do you think he's nervous as well?" she asked.

"Not at all," Marcia assured her. "I'm sure he puts his shirt on inside out all the time! Putting pepper on his oatmeal is a common practice as well, I understand!"

"Is she up yet?" Zillah peeked in the door. "We are going to be late to the church, and if we are, then we shall be late coming back to the house, and all of the food will be ruined!" Fan, Adah, and Annis followed Zillah into the room. Fan had a basket of freshly picked flowers for the bridesmaids' hair.

Marcia helped Millie wash up and dress, and Aunt Wealthy sent Adah to bring the curling iron that had been heating on the stove. She pressed ringlets into Millie's hair, and caught it up on her head with wisps of curls about her face.

102

"Now sit in that chair and don't move a muscle until we have the girls dressed," Aunt Wealthy said.

Marcia had agreed to allow all the girls, even Annis, to wear their hair up, so Aunt Wealthy set to work with the iron, curling their hair after Marcia put their gowns on them. Annis was so delighted with her bouncing curls and her flaring skirt that she kept twirling and bumping into things until Marcia made her sit by Millie. Adah was the last to have her hair done, and she was quite ready to sit in the chair and let herself be pampered after having run the curling iron up and down the stairs for heating on the stove. Fan twined crowns of flowers for her sisters' hair.

"You should have a piece of toast before we go," Zillah said to Millie. "It will settle your stomach."

"Nothing could settle my stomach," Millie said. "It feels as if an army of caterpillars is on parade."

"All right, then, just let me make sure Charles isn't looking." Zillah peeked out the bedroom door. "No one in sight," she said. "Ru promised he would keep them in the kitchen until we were away."

Millie and Zillah crept down the stairs and out the front door where a coach decorated with white ribbons and bells was waiting to carry Millie, Marcia, and the girls to the church. Charles, Otis, and the boys would follow in a second coach.

"You mustn't stay and talk after the ceremony," Marcia said, as they started with a lurch. "Everyone will be at the house half an hour later for the wedding breakfast, and you and Charles must be there to greet them."

Jasmine and Runhilda were at the church already, dressed in their bridesmaids gowns, fresh flowers twined in their hair. Most of the guests were seated, all in their

Millie's Reluctant Sacrifice

Sunday best for the wedding. The church itself had not been decorated, save for a white ribbon on the altar. Millie saw the edge of John Q. Landreth's frame at the end of a pew. Mrs. Prior was standing in front of it, her arms folded as if she had been arguing with the old man.

"This is a most peculiar practice, if you ask me," she said as Millie walked up. "Having portraits of dead folk at your wedding. I've never heard of such a thing. I'm not sure we should have portraits in church at all. They're graven images, if you ask me." John Q. looked as disgruntled as Mrs. Prior sounded. "I sure don't know why he has to sit at the end of my pew!"

"It's probably a southern custom," Mrs. Monocker said, "having such things at a wedding."

"I don't think so," Marcia said. "I believe it is peculiar to Otis Lochneer."

"I see," Mrs. Prior sniffed. "I think I'll have a talk with that young man, Marcia. We could drag this out of here right now—"

"Too late. The groom's here!" Adah announced from the window.

The caterpillars in Millie's stomach hatched into full-grown butterflies when she saw Charles step out of the coach. He looked very fine in a mulberry frock coat and trousers of lavender doeskin. Otis had clearly tied his cravat. Millie felt a flash of panic. *What if Helen is right? Is this dress too simple for marriage to a doctor?*

"Get out of sight!" Zillah said, pushing Millie toward the door to the Sunday school room. "He's coming!" The bridesmaids hurried in behind her, and Aunt Wealthy checked each one to make sure they were in order, tucking a drooping flower back into Jasmine's crown and brushing a spot of lint from Annis's sleeve.

"Millie, you are gorgeous!" Fan gasped as Aunt Wealthy draped the lace veil over her. "The most beautiful bride Pleasant Plains has ever seen!"

Celestia Ann agreed, peeking in the door. "Come on, ladies." The bridesmaids went out one by one. "Now don't be nervous," Celestia Ann said with a wink as she closed the door.

Millie stood for what seemed an eternity in the Sunday school room until Aunt Wealthy beckoned her out. Stuart, smiling, was waiting for her at the back of the church. Millie took his arm, he patted her arm, and they started down the aisle. Ahead, Charles was waiting for her in front of the altar, Otis and her brothers at his side. The bridesmaids had stopped giggling and were looking very serious indeed as Stuart gave Millie's hand to Charles, and went to sit by Marcia.

"You look beautiful," Charles whispered.

"I do?" Millie said, her voice much louder than she intended.

"We are not to that part yet," Reverend Lord said, flipping through his book of prayers.

Annis giggled. Millie tried to blink her to silence, but it only made the girl giggle more. Cyril was having a hard time keeping his laughter in, and Charles was looking with some alarm at his bride's fluttering eyelashes. Otis started blinking as well, apparently trying to control his expression and failing.

"Ah! Here we are." Reverend Lord had found the right page. He bowed his head, and suddenly, in the silence, the room was filled with the presence of God, as deep and still and joyful as Millie had ever felt it.

Millie's Reluctant Sacrifice

"Do you, Charles Landreth, promise to love this woman?" Reverend Lord asked.

"I do," Charles said. "I commit to love her as Christ loves the church, giving myself up to make her holy."

"And do you, Millie Keith, agree to submit to this man as to the Lord?"

"I do," Millie said. "Where you go, Charles, I will go, and where you stay, I will stay. Your people will be my people and your God my God. Where you die I will die, and there I will be buried."

"Then before the Lord and all his angels," Reverend Lord said, "I pronounce you man and wife."

Good-byes and Good Advice

Listen to advice and accept
instruction, and in the end
you will be wise.

PROVERBS 19:20

*T*he house on Keith Hill had been transformed with white bows on every door and window. A garden arbor decorated with satin bows and doves sheltered a table with three cakes: a rich wedding fruitcake with cream icing, a white bride's cake, and a chocolate groom's cake.

The guests began arriving almost as soon as Millie and Charles stepped from the carriage. Adah was put in charge of keeping little fingers out of the orange blossoms and roses made of icing on the cakes, shooing the children away until they had eaten breakfast.

There were far too many guests to sit at one table or even in one room, so the reception spilled out over the porches and into the gardens. Millie let go of Charles's arm for one moment, and he was lost in the crowd. Even on tiptoe, she couldn't see him. Otis was in the corner, setting the portrait of John Q. up on a chair where it could glower over the crowd. Mrs. Prior was helping him maneuver the canvas and frame, but Charles was nowhere to be seen.

The food smelled wonderful, and Millie tried to make her way through the crowd toward a table laden with eggs, sausages, and muffins, but everyone had a word of congratulations and best wishes for the bride. Many were hearing for the first time that Millie was leaving Pleasant Plains that very day, so there were tears along with the laughter.

Millie had just reached the table when Damaris Ransquate caught her arm, half dragging her across the room to a quiet corner. "Millie," she said, shaking her head, "I don't have the words. I wouldn't be a Christian today if it wasn't for your witness. I'm going to miss you so much!"

"I'll miss you too." Millie hugged her friend, hoping Damaris did not hear her stomach growl. "And I want you to know that you are doing an excellent job with little Runhilda."

"That child is a gift from God," Damaris said. "A gift."

Millie agreed, and then turned to find her friend Lucilla at her shoulder. "Bolivia!" Lu cried. "Millie, how could you? Africa is so far away!"

By the time Millie had rearranged the continents for Lu, Annis was tugging on her skirt. "Mamma says it's time to cut the cake!" she said. "And I get to pull a ribbon, Millie!"

Millie looked longingly at the tables of food as Annis dragged her past them. She was happy to find Charles waiting for her by the cake. They cut the wedding cake together, his hand on hers, and put pieces in boxes for the wedding party to take home. Millie resisted the urge to lick the icing from her fingers only because her Sunday school class was watching. The bride's cake was next, and her bridesmaids gathered around giggling, waiting to pull one of the ribbons from beneath the cake to see which charm it held.

"May I go first?" Annis asked, stepping forward. She looked at the ribbons around the base of the cake, and then at Fan. "Tell me the rhyme again," she said.

"The ring for marriage within a year," Fan quoted,
"The penny for wealth, my dear,
The thimble for an old maid born,
The button for sweethearts all forlorn."

"I changed my mind," Annis said. "You go first, Adah. You are the oldest."

Adah stepped up to the cake, chose a ribbon, and pulled out her charm—a small golden ring.

"Marriage within a year!" Fan exclaimed. "It's good that you chose that one, Adah. None of the rest of us are old enough."

"I'm not, either," Adah replied, but she slipped the ring in her pocket.

The ribbon Annis chose was tied to a penny. Fan seemed pleased enough to draw the thimble, but Jasmine's button was nothing less than a tragedy. "I'm not a sweetheart," she insisted. "I want the thimble!" Fan would not trade, saying she would rather be an old maid than forlorn, sweetheart or not.

As soon as the boxes of cake were handed out, Millie took Charles's arm and they started for the buffet table, but Dr. Chetwood stepped in front of them. Mrs. Chetwood put a glass of lemonade in Millie's hand as Dr. Chetwood handed Charles another.

"A toast to the young couple!" Dr. Chetwood said, and everyone raised cups and glasses. "I can think of no better advice than was given by Benjamin Franklin to a newly married friend: 'Treat your wife always with respect; it will procure respect to you, not from her only, but from all that observe it. Never use a slight expression to her, even in jest, for slights in jest, after frequent bandying, are apt to end in angry earnest. Be studious in your profession, and you will be learned. Be industrious and frugal, and you will be rich. Be sober and temperate, and you will be healthy. Be in general virtuous, and you will be happy.'" He started to drink, but Frank Osborne cleared his throat.

"I believe Mr. Franklin went on to say: 'I pray God to bless you both!'" said Frank.

Millie's Reluctant Sacrifice

Dr. Chetwood raised his eyebrows. "A scholar, I see. Then in the name of good scholarship and historical accuracy, I will add: I pray God to bless you both!"

The cool lemonade only made Millie's stomach growl more loudly, but she was sure no one could hear it over the noise and gaiety.

"It's time to go, Charles," Otis said, looking at his watch. "The stage leaves at noon." Millie handed Charles her glass, then hurried to her room to change into her traveling dress and pick up her carpetbag and parasol.

Their friends lined the path to the carriage, and Millie and Charles said good-bye to each and every one again.

"He's not so bad after all," Mrs. Prior said, dabbing her eyes as Millie said good-bye.

"Do you mean Otis?" Charles asked.

"Your great-grandfather. I could get used to a face like that. In fact, if you ever need a place for him, send him to me. I'll hang him in the dinin' room. People will mind their manners then, I imagine!"

Millie's Sunday school class was the last to say good-bye, all standing by the carriage with tears in their eyes.

"Who's going to teach us?" Runhilda asked.

"Adah will," Millie said. "And she is a very good teacher. Since you are all very good students, I'm sure it will be a happy match."

Charles started to lift her into the carriage amidst a chorus of "Good-bye, Miss Keith, good-bye teacher," when she caught sight of a pale, sad face at the back of the crowd.

"Just a moment, Charles," Millie said, and he set her down again. She opened her arms just in time to catch the little girl.

"Millie! I don't want you to go," she sobbed. "I want to keep you forever, no matter what Miss Stanhope says."

Good-byes and Good Advice

"I want to keep you, too. Here," she held out her purple parasol. Jaz had to let go of Millie's waist to take it. "If I do not come home, you must promise to bring this to me one day, Jasmine Mikolaus."

"I promise," Jaz said, clutching it to her breast. "No matter how far, Millie. I'll come as soon as I am grown."

Charles handed Millie into the carriage, and they waved good-bye to Keith Hill. Millie had barely time enough to compose herself before she had more good-byes to say at the stage station, as her family had followed the carriage to town. Her sisters hugged her and her brothers kissed her cheek and shook Charles's hand as their trunks were being loaded onto the stage.

"Well!" Aunt Wealthy said. "I want you to know, Charles, that I am proud of you. It is a wonderful thing to have a Doctor of Medical Science in the family, and you have done well with your studies and your practice. Now you must work on your true calling: a Professor-of-Christ. And remember, both of you, that no matter where you go, there is someone praying for you."

"God bless you and be with you," Stuart said, gripping Charles's hand. "And take care of our little girl."

Marcia had tears in her eyes as Millie kissed her good-bye. "Don't cry, Mamma," she said. "It won't be forever."

"Ah, Millie," Marcia said. "You were born for adventure, and I am quite willing to give you up to God...but I would have loved a few more years with you."

"I'll take good care of her," Charles said, shaking Stuart's hand.

"See that you do, young man, and may God take care of you both."

113

Millie's Reluctant Sacrifice

The driver was tapping his toe with impatience. "Aren't you folks done yet? I got a schedule to keep here."

Cyril smiled at him. "I don't think you should be so eager to leave," he said. "Not with my sister on board. Things seem to happen when she travels—people catching fire on trains, steamboats hitting sandbars."

"Cyril!" Millie glared at him. "Those are perfectly normal occurrences. Well, possibly not bustles igniting on trains. But steamboats often run aground on sandbars. And that was years and years ago."

"Stage drivers dropping dead," Cyril added.

The stagecoach driver stopped his work to look at her. "You're Millie Keith, ain't you? I heard about that."

"She's Millie Landreth," Charles said, taking her hand. "And you have nothing to fear, sir. There is a doctor on board."

The driver slammed the door behind them. They were the only passengers, it seemed, as Otis would be leaving on a later stage, planning to settle his affairs in North Carolina and then meet them in New York in time to sail.

Millie leaned out the window. "Good-bye!" she called, then grabbed her hat as the stage started forward with a jolt.

The driver was determined to make up for lost time, racing through town at a breakneck speed, causing Charles and Millie to cling to the doors, seats, and each other, or risk bouncing off the ceilings and walls. The horses were unable to keep up the pace for more than a few miles, and they eventually settled into a slower gait.

As soon as they stopped their wild careening, Charles reached into his pocket and pulled out a linen napkin, which he spread on Millie's lap. Next he opened his carpetbag, and out came boiled eggs, muffins, and a jar of buttermilk.

"Charles," Millie said, "have I told you recently how much I love you?"

"Not recently enough. But it would never do to have my wife starve to death on our wedding day. We'll have to drink from the jar, I'm afraid. I didn't want to take any of your mother's cups."

"It's fortunate, then, that we are the only passengers," she laughed.

They had finished their meal and tucked the scraps away before the stage stopped at a crossroads to pick up a farmer and his wife.

"Where's you off to?" the woman asked.

"We are going to Bolivia," Millie explained. "My husband," the words seemed strange on her tongue, "has been offered a job there as a doctor at a mining company."

"Bolivia!" The thin woman's eyes grew large. "I had a cousin went to Bolivia. They et him."

"Now, Ma," the fat man corrected. "That warn't Boliviar a-tall. That was some island off of Floridee."

"Same sort of savages!" the woman said, shaking her head. "You've no children, have you? Well, that's a blessing. It's a hard world for orphans, that's the plain and simple truth. Now, I'm not lying," she said to her husband who was trying to shush her. "Orphans have a hard lot!"

"Delphinia don't mean to be bold," the man said. "She's had a hard life, and hates to see anyone suffer. You say you're a doctor, young man?"

"Yes," Charles said.

"Well then, you should be just the man I want to talk to. Imagine me sitting right here beside you! That's providence, that's what it is!"

"Do you have a medical problem?" Charles asked.

Millie's Reluctant Sacrifice

"Me! No, not me. I'm as healthy as they come. But I got sheep that I could use some advice about."

"Sheep." Charles glanced at Millie. She tried not to smile.

"Yessir, sheep. I know they are rare in these parts, but my cousin has had good results with them, real good, so I thought I would get me a few. The trouble is, they got runny noses."

"I...there were very few sheep in Chicago where I learned my practice," Charles said. "I worked primarily on humans."

"Can't be that different," the farmer said. "What do you expect is ailin' my sheep?"

"Grub-in-nose," Millie said. "They've got fly larva in their snouts."

"You don't say!" The farmer never took his eyes off of Charles. "What do I do about it?"

"Rub a little tar around their nostrils," Millie said. "It will keep the flies from laying eggs."

"There!" The farmer slapped his knee. "I knew you was the man to ask! Didn't I tell you, wife? That's what education will do for a man! So you're gonna doctor people in Bolivia?"

"Actually," Charles said, "I'm going to tell them about Jesus. Do you—"

"Now see here," the farmer's face grew red. "Sheeps' snouts is one thing, but a man's religion is another. I'm as good as any other man, I guess, and I don't need you shoving your religion on me!"

He turned his face to the wall, and his wife dropped her eyes to her hands, which were fidgeting in her lap. They did not say another word all the way to the next town where they left the stage. The farmer stuck his head back in the door, after his wife was out.

"Thank you for the ad-vice, young feller," he said. "But you've got to learn not to talk about God so much. People should be private about that kind of thing."

"Well," Charles said to Millie, shaking his head. "I guess I have failed my first assignment as a Professor-of-Christ. I didn't get two words out. And how did you know—"

"About grub-in-nose? I read a book about sheep once," Millie said.

CHAPTER

9

Divine
Appointments

*But in your hearts set apart Christ
as Lord. Always be prepared to
give an answer to everyone
who asks you to give the
reason for the hope that
you have.*

1 PETER 3:15

Divine Appointments

*I*n two weeks of travel by stage and by rail, Millie and Charles had encountered not one difficulty. The weather was good, the stages were on time, and the conductors were whistling and cheerful. *Perhaps becoming Mrs. Landreth has changed something, Lord,* Millie prayed.

She looked back down the platform to where Charles stood talking earnestly with two university students they had met on the train, and her brow furrowed. They had seemed like very polite young men, discussing church with Millie, but when Charles had accompanied them into the dining hall at the last station, he had returned with a troubled look on his face. He had been very quiet that afternoon, and Millie saw him taking special note of Ephesians 4:29–30. She didn't have to read over his shoulder to know what he was pondering. It was one of the first verses her mother had given her to memorize: *Do not let any unwholesome talk come out of your mouths, but only what is helpful for building others up according to their needs, that it may benefit those who listen. And do not grieve the Holy Spirit of God, with whom you were sealed for the day of redemption.*

When the train stopped again, Charles had asked her if he could have a moment to speak with the young men alone, and the moment had turned into half an hour. Now he had his pocket Bible in his hand, showing the taller of the two a verse. The man shook his head, and the other laughed and slapped Charles on the back, as if he had told a joke.

Lord, give him the right words to speak, Millie prayed quietly to herself. *I am so proud that he will stand up for You and for what is right!* Charles had been doing just that since they had left

121

Millie's Reluctant Sacrifice

Pleasant Plains. "If I'm called to be a missionary," he said, "I see no point in waiting. People here and now are dying without knowing Jesus." Millie heartily agreed, but Charles had received amused smiles, lectures on his manners, and advice to keep such things in church "where they belong."

"All aboard that's getting aboard!" the conductor called, and Millie made her way back down the track. The students had already boarded.

"I must confess something to you, wife," Charles said when he joined her. "I have been a Christian for four years, and I have never seen anyone come to a saving faith in Jesus. I have not even been able to convince my best friend, Otis, and all the while I read accounts of great evangelists who simply walked into a building and people would fall to their knees."

Millie sat on the hard train seat, scooting toward the window to make room for him. "And I have read of missionaries who labored for twenty years before they saw their first convert," Millie said as he sat down. "God uses those who persevere. His Spirit seems to move on the most unlikely people, at the most unlikely times as well."

"That is comforting," Charles said sadly. "I am beginning to feel like a most unlikely missionary. I would truly like to see one—just one—touched by the saving grace of God before I leave to be a missionary on foreign soil."

Charles rested his head in his hands, and Millie knew that he was praying silently, pouring out his frustration to the One who loved him best. She put her hand on his shoulder. *Father*, she prayed, *send Charles a divine appointment. Let Your Spirit lead him to the people You want him to speak to. Encourage him, Lord.*

Divine Appointments

They took a hansom cab from the train station to the hotel at which Otis had made reservations for them. Millie had to resist the urge to lean out the window and stare. She felt as if she had come to the land of giants, of Sara and Angelina Grimke, of Frank Lloyd Garrison, and so many other great names in the nation's history that Millie could not imagine them all in one place at one time. New York was their city, and they filled it from edge to edge in Millie's mind, but it wasn't giants she saw on the streets. It was laborers, laundresses, and street urchins wherever she looked. Barefoot boys in ragged shirts sold newspapers on the corners, shouting out headlines; girls sold flowers and apples; crowds flowed back and forth around them. Little children played along the sidewalks and in the streets, between buildings that formed the horizons of their world. Millie tried to imagine Annis and Jaz playing here, but she could not picture them trapped between the rows of buildings with only sidewalks and cobblestone on which to play.

"Mrs. and Mrs. Landreth," the woman at the desk of the hotel said, checking her registry. "Yes, I have your reservations. Two weeks, paid in full." She smiled, and her cheeks puckered into autumn apples, wrinkled but rosy with rouge. Millie was fascinated by her face. It was almost beautiful, almost young, dusted with powder and touched with paint. "Nothing is too good for friends of Mr. Lochneer. I'll show you to your suite myself. Are you traveling with a maid?"

When Millie said that she was not, the woman shook her head. "I will send a girl to iron and hang your clothes. You had a long trip and must be exhausted."

Millie's Reluctant Sacrifice

She took a key from a board beneath the desk, then led them down the hall and up three flights of stairs, finally opening the door to an elegant sitting room. There were two doors opposite the one they entered, one opening to reveal a water closet complete with a tub standing on lions' paws, and the other a bedroom with a window that over-looked the city.

"Mr. Sauer liked this room," she said. "He liked to look out the window."

"I can see why." Charles moved aside so that Millie could look out as well. The street was a dizzying four stories below.

"It's like a parade," the woman said, "with the latest fashion for ladies and gents marching by. I've watched it for years. Fashions for the beggars and paupers don't change much over time." Her voice was sad. "They tend to be thin, ragged, and dull, year in and year out."

She's like a late summer flower, refusing to yield to the frost, Millie thought. She decided suddenly that she liked this woman.

"Will these rooms be sufficient?" the woman asked.

"Yes, they are lovely," Millie said. "Thank you, Miss. . . ?"

"Oh." The autumn apples appeared again. "I forgot, didn't I? It's Mrs., not Miss. Mrs. Sauer."

"Oh, I'm sorry," Millie said.

"Sorry?" She looked alarmed. "Then the rooms are not to your liking?"

"Of course they are," Millie assured her. "I'm sorry for the loss of your husband."

"Oh, Hans is not dead. He's travelling on the continent . . .just travelling. Here are your trunks. Now, if you freshen up quickly, you have time to take in a play at Covent Garden. *London Assurance* is getting excellent reviews."

Divine Appointments

When they returned from the theatre, their clothing was ironed and hung in the closets, and a light evening snack of jellyrolls and tea waited in their room. The maid must have run up the back stairs with it as soon as they came in the building's front door, as the tea was piping hot.

"I think I could grow used to this part of being a missionary," Charles said, patting the goose down comforter on the bed. He had changed his mind by one o'clock in the morning, however. Neither of them had slept a wink. The sound of carriage wheels and horses' hooves in the street below their room—a clipping, clopping, and rattling riot—seemed to go on all night.

∽

"I feel as if I would frighten a small child," Millie said as they sat down to breakfast in the hotel dining room the next morning. Her eyes felt gritty and swollen from lack of sleep.

"Nonsense," Charles said, peering sleepily across the table at her. "Well…"

"Well?"

"Children adore raccoons," he laughed.

"Was it too noisy for you?" Mrs. Sauer stopped by their table. "Fifteen years ago, when we bought the hotel, New York was a town of sixty thousand souls. Now, the paper says that three hundred thousand people call this city home. The sound of that many people living and breathing can drive a person insane." She leaned closer. "That's what drove Hans away, I expect." She stood silent for a moment. "I'll tell you what. If you have a riding habit, Mrs. Landreth, I'll direct you to where you can have some peace. There are quiet neighborhoods in New York, if you know where to find them!"

Millie's Reluctant Sacrifice

Right after breakfast Millie changed into her riding habit, and Mrs. Sauer led them to the alley behind the hotel. There was a small shed under the back steps. She opened the door and waved at two very strange contraptions leaning against the wall. Each had two wheels of equal size and a seat between them. One wheel could clearly be turned by means of handlebars on top. The whole thing, seat to wheels, was made of wood.

"It's a Laufmaschine—a running machine," Mrs. Sauer said. "It was invented by my husband's uncle, Baron Karl Friedrich Drais von Sauerbronn. He had extensive gardens, and this device helped him get around them faster. My husband is royal all the way back on the German side."

"A hobbyhorse!" Charles said.

"Some people call it that," Mrs. Sauer said, "but that's not the correct name. An inventor should be able to name his own invention, don't you think?"

"May I?" Charles straddled one of the contraptions and pushed himself along for a few feet. "It's marvelous! How do you stop?"

"Put your feet down," Mrs. Sauer said. "You may have to drag them. Mr. Sauer and I ran all over New York City on these machines, in happier days."

It was clear to Millie that her boots were not suitable for travel by hobbyhorse, so she changed into more sturdy walking shoes. Mrs. Sauer ordered a picnic basket packed for them and drew them a map. Charles hung the basket on the handles of his hobbyhorse, and they set off cautiously down the street—each of them on their own hobbyhorse.

"Have fun," Mrs. Sauer called after them. Millie quickly got the hang of riding her hobbyhorse. It was like running, only when you grew tired, you could pick up your feet and glide forward—so long as you kept your balance. Hobbyhorses were apparently not well known in New York, as people pointed, stopped, and stared.

They had gone perhaps a mile when they encountered a small upward incline in the street. This was harder going, and Millie was glad when they reached the top of the hill. "Walking would be easier than this," she puffed over her shoulder.

"Millie, don't—" Charles said as she gave her hobbyhorse a push, relieved that she could just sit on the seat and glide. The rest of his words were lost behind her as the hobbyhorse suddenly began rushing down the hill.

"Look out!" Millie tried to shout at the people on the street ahead of her, but the wooden wheels on the cobblestones were making her teeth chatter. She put her feet down, but she was moving much too quickly now, and the leather soles of her shoes merely skidded along. The wind from the speed of her ride pulled her cap from her head.

"Charrrleeeee!" she cried, but she could not look back to see if he was behind her. "Lord, help meee-eeek!"

Miraculously, the pedestrians seemed to know she was coming—a sea of people parting before her. Millie had glimpses of startled faces as she shot past, and then the street was climbing again, and the hobbyhorse slowed enough for Millie to jump off. She found herself in the center of a group of curious onlookers. Her hair had come undone and was falling over her face, but she saw Charles, running beside his hobbyhorse. He held the contraption with both hands, and her cap, which he must have stopped to rescue, was in his teeth.

Millie pulled her hair back into a bun and tried to secure it with the few pins that were left after the riotous ride, very much aware that she was a spectacle, and laughing in spite of herself.

Millie's Reluctant Sacrifice

"A Laufmaschine!" a voice said in delight. "Miss, if I might just sit on it for a moment. I have made it my ambition and my goal to travel the world by every means of transportation invented by God or by man!"

Millie stopped searching for pins. The voice was familiar, and the sentiment more familiar still. She turned around and around, but she could not see any familiar face in the crowd that had formed. "Colonel?" she called. "Colonel Peabody? Is that you?"

An elderly man with mutton chops pushed his way through the crowd. He adjusted his spectacles and peered at her face.

"Why, Millie Keith! If I hadn't been so keen on observing your manner of conveyance, I would have recognized you at once!"

Charles finally reached them, and the crowd, seeing that she was not going to provide any more entertainment, drifted away.

"You remember my speaking of Colonel Peabody?" she asked Charles. "The gentleman who first suggested we could sneak Luke out of the South in a coffin? This is the very man himself!"

"I don't believe we had the pleasure of a formal introduction," the Colonel said, inclining his head. It was easy to see that he was fascinated by the running machines. "These devices—are they yours?"

"We have borrowed them," Millie said. "Would you like to try one? It seems quite safe if there are no hills."

The colonel traded his top hat for her hobbyhorse, and, perching on the seat, he ran with great, swinging strides down the level street and back again.

"Marvelous," he said when he returned. "Simply marvelous." He took a notepad and pencil nub from his pocket. "My brain has started to leak," he explained, "and so I must make notes. If I do not, I will not remember which adventures to convey to Opal and Ruth.

"Miz Opal and Ruth!" Millie cried. "Are they in town?"

"They are, and can you believe? They have recently accused me of making up tales. They will never believe this, I assure you. That I met Millie Keith and rode a Laufmaschine."

"It's Millie Landreth now, but if you will allow me, I would be delighted to provide proof," Millie said. He handed her the pad, and she wrote a brief note expressing a desire to see them while she was in town.

"Are Luke and Laylie still with you?" Millie asked. "I long to see Laylie again."

"Who?" The Colonel seemed truly puzzled. He pulled out his watch and looked at it. "I'm late! They will start without me," he said, and taking his hat back from Millie, he hurried away.

"Do you think he will give them your note?" Charles asked.

"I hope so," Millie said. "Imagine, finding the Colonel in the middle of three hundred thousand people!"

Re-boarding their hobbyhorses, they continued on for another half mile before they reached their destination.

"Have you noticed that the proprietress of our hotel is a very strange woman?" Charles asked, stopping by an iron gate. Mrs. Sauer's "quiet neighborhood" was very quiet indeed. The good woman had directed them to the Greenwood Cemetery.

"It is peaceful," Millie said, pulling the gate open.

Millie's Reluctant Sacrifice

The only other living soul was an ancient gardener who could have doubled as a scarecrow made of sticks and bones. His clothing was colorless with washing and age, and he frowned at them as they walked by. He was busily clipping the grass around the headstones with long-bladed shears. He seemed drawn to work close to the two visitors so Millie invited him to join them, but he only grunted, turning his back as Millie spread their picnic. The only sound as they ate was the clipping and snipping of the shears.

"It is peaceful," Charles said, "though a strange place for a meal."

"I wonder if they knew Jesus," Millie said. "The people who are buried here, I mean." *Clang!* Millie glanced at the gardener. His shears had hit a stone. "These are the people of New York City," Millie continued, "who walked the streets and laughed and went to the theatre. I wonder if anyone told them about Jesus. And think of all the others living here now, three hundred thousand men, women, and children! Full of the busyness of life. They will be here soon, too. I wonder if they ever think of it."

"Hmmm..." A mumble came from the direction of the gardener.

"Hmmm?" Millie looked up from putting the plates back in the basket.

"A very strange Scripture just came to mind," Charles said as he took his small Bible out of his pocket and flipped it open. "I can hear it in my head, but I can't remember where it is. Ah, I've got it—Ezekiel 37: "The hand of the Lord was upon me," he read, "and he brought me out by the Spirit of the Lord and set me in the middle of a valley; it was full of bones."

Charles seemed unaware that the sound of the shears had stopped completely, and the gardener leaned his head against the tombstone as Charles continued: "He led me back and forth among them, and I saw a great many bones on the floor of the valley, bones that were very dry. He asked me, 'Son of man, can these bones live?' I said, 'O Sovereign Lord, you alone know.' "

There was a low groan, and Charles looked up.

"Keep reading," Millie whispered, and Charles went on: "Then he said to me, 'Prophesy to these bones and say to them, "Dry bones, hear the word of the Lord! This is what the Sovereign Lord says to these bones: I will make breath enter you, and you will come to life. I will attach tendons to you and make flesh come upon you and cover you with skin; I will put breath in you, and you will come to life. Then you will know that I am the Lord." '

"O God!" the old man cried suddenly. "I am a sinful man, a bag of dead bones. Can you give life to me? I am a sinner worthy of death!"

Millie went to stand beside him. "Jesus will take those sins, if you ask Him," she said gently. "He wants to give you new life."

"Then he said to me," Charles came over to them, still reading, " 'Prophesy to the breath; prophesy, son of man, and say to it, "This is what the Sovereign Lord says: Come from the four winds, O breath, and breathe into these slain, that they may live." ' "

The old man was sobbing now, his shoulders shaking, and his nose running. Millie gave him her handkerchief and he hid his face in it.

"It's too late, too late," he said. "Why would God want me now? I am just dry, dry bones."

Millie's Reluctant Sacrifice

Charles laid his hand on the man's head. " 'I will put my Spirit in you,' " he read, " 'and you will live.' "

"Aaaaahhhh!" the old man cried. He fell to his knees. "I want to live. If You can take these sins, Jesus, take them, take them, take them!" He was quiet so long that Millie and Charles began to worry, but at last he looked up.

"It's true," he said. "I know it. He has taken them. Show me where you were reading. Show me the words." Charles handed the old man the Bible, and he held it at arm's length to read the words. " 'Then you, my people, will know that I am the Lord,' " he read. "I know the Lord! Thank You, Jesus!" Suddenly, he started running.

"Where are you going?" Charles called after him.

"To tell my brother," the man said. "He's got to know, too!"

"That was the most amazing thing I have ever seen," Millie said, flushed with the joy of the Lord.

Charles's face was glowing. "It was a miracle!" Charles said. "God gave me that Scripture, Millie. I know it. There were chills running up and down my whole body as I read. Come on!" he said, picking up his hobbyhorse. "We have to find a bookstore."

"A bookstore?" Millie questioned him, confused.

"He took my Bible with him," Charles said with a smile.

⌒

"I'm so glad we ran into the Colonel," Millie said as they waited for the door to open. "I had no hope of ever seeing Miz Opal, and I have wanted so badly to know what became of Luke and Laylie." There had been a card waiting for them when they returned to the hotel the day before, inviting them to tea.

"Millie!" Miz Opal opened her door wide, and showed them into a simple room. "I am delighted to see you! And Charles Landreth! We heard that you had left the South, but I never imagined I would be entertaining you in my home! Come in!"

Millie was hugged and kissed by Miz Opal and Miz Ruth, and Colonel Peabody shook Charles's hand at least twice. Dearest and Blessed Bliss were doing well, their funeral parlor doing a steady if not lively business.

"I wish I could tell you more," Miz Opal said when Millie asked after Luke and Laylie. "They stayed with me for two years. Laylie taught her brother to read."

Miz Ruth fluttered her hand. "I have never seen anything like it. He memorized the entire New Testament. The entire thing, word for word!"

"You know a black man cannot travel with a book," Miz Opal said. "Luke decided he would have to *be* the book—be the Gospel—to his people in the south. He tried to leave Laylie behind, but she would not be left. We have not heard a word from them for years now."

"They are in great danger, if they still live," Miss Ruth said. "I would have done anything I could to make them stay, but they believed it was the Lord calling them to His work."

"To their deaths, more likely," the Colonel said. "We should have stopped them, or I should have gone with them."

"Luke was not afraid to die for the Lord," Miz Opal said simply. "Nor was Laylie. They knew what they were facing better than we ever can, dear."

Miss Ruth wiped her eyes. "I understand Luke being called. But why Laylie? Why couldn't she stay at home?"

Millie's Reluctant Sacrifice

"In Christ there is no male or female," Miz Opal said, "but we are all heirs according to the promise. How can we keep it to ourselves? Did our Lord not tell each and every one of us to take the Gospel to the world?"

CHAPTER 10

A Piece of Wood

For the message of the cross is foolishness to those who are perishing, but to us who are being saved it is the power of God.

1 CORINTHIANS 1:18

A Piece of Wood

*T*he following Sunday Colonel Peabody invited them to attend church with him. Millie was glad to accept the invitation, and gladder still when she sat surrounded by more Christians in one place than she had ever seen before, rich and poor gathered together. The church itself was a fortress, but the grey stone exterior it showed the world gave no hint of the warmth Millie found inside. Light streamed through stained glass, shining on the brass pipes of an immense organ. The pastor, an elderly man, gave an eloquent sermon on Isaiah 50:4. "The Sovereign Lord has given me an instructed tongue, to know the word that sustains the weary. He wakens me morning by morning, wakens my ear to listen like one being taught." Millie made a note to herself to memorize the beautiful verse.

As three hundred voices lifted in song, Charles leaned close to her ear. "I believe this is what Heaven will be like," he whispered. "Wall-to-wall joy and floor-to-ceiling hallelujahs!"

"I hope it has a pipe organ!" Millie whispered back. She had forgotten how much she missed playing piano until the first sweet note had sounded. Now she closed her eyes and listened with every fiber, as if she could soak the music up and take it with her.

Otis arrived near the end of their two weeks in New York, and the process of purchasing medical supplies for the clinic began, although they had to arrange for delivery at a later date. The *Annabelle Lee*, the ship they were to sail on, had not made port and was a full two weeks overdue.

Millie's Reluctant Sacrifice

The two weeks turned to three, and one morning Mrs. Sauer brought a message to their breakfast table and handed it to Otis. He paled slightly as he read it.

"I believe we will have to make new accommodations for our travel," he said. "The *Annabelle Lee* was lost at sea with all hands."

"How horrible!" Millie set her fork down. "I think we should pray for the families of the drowned sailors and for ourselves. If we delay much longer, the weather will turn foul."

"You may pray." Otis dabbed his lips with a napkin. "But I believe taking decisive action is of more avail."

"You don't believe in prayer, then?" Millie asked.

Otis looked at Charles and flushed slightly. "I have no arguments with those who do," he said. "But I'm afraid my experience has led me to the conclusion that Christianity is very much like the story of Aladdin and the magic lamp."

"Aladdin?" Millie was truly mystified.

Otis pursed his lips. "Aladdin had a genie, did he not?" Millie nodded. "And he kept him in a bottle. When he wanted a wish granted, he rubbed the lamp, and the genie came out. Christians have a God, and they keep him in the church. When they want a wish granted, they rub their hands together," he put his palms together as if he were praying, "and make their wish!"

"That is not at all what Christians are doing!" Millie began, but Otis only shrugged.

"Whatever the case, my uncle's money is the genie in my lamp. I'm going to the office of the shipping company to see if rubbing it on some palms will produce a ship."

"I believe I will go with you," Charles said. "That is, if Millie doesn't mind."

A Piece of Wood

Millie did not and was in fact glad for the time alone — or at least without Otis. She gathered her bonnet and reticule and started down the street, praying as she went. *Aladdin's genie indeed! Father, I know You love Otis and want him to be with You forever, but I confess, two months on a ship seems very much like an eternity to me. He is a mocker, and if there is one serious bone in his body, I don't know where he keeps it! Give me patience, Lord.*

A young woman gave her a startled look, grabbed her little daughter's hand, and hurried away. Millie marched on, praying under her breath for Otis, for Charles, and for herself, that she would have a sweet, calm spirit, and that they would have success in finding a ship.

When all of the starch had gone out of her at last, and all of the prayer as well, she found herself standing in front of a window full of darling bonnets. She wandered into the shop and wandered out half an hour later with a new parasol. The weight of it on her arm reminded her of Jasmine, and a flood of homesickness rolled over her. And so she found herself praying her way up the street again toward the hotel, this time for all the girls in her Sunday school class in Pleasant Plains.

Mrs. Sauer was at the front desk. "You were so kind to allow us to use your Laufmaschine," Millie said. "And we have never properly thanked you. I want to leave a note for Mr. Sauer as well."

Mrs. Sauer's face trembled. "I must tell you a secret," she said. "Mr. Sauer is not visiting the continent. He is dead." She put her hand over her mouth, closing her eyes for a moment. "You are the first person I have ever said that to. I heard what you were talking about with Otis, and I believe in God. Will you…remember me in prayer?"

Millie's Reluctant Sacrifice

"Of course, I will!" Millie assured her. "Do you—forgive me, but you seem very lonely. Do you have any friends in the city?"

"Not since Mr. Sauer went away. I haven't been invited out much."

"I have some friends here that I'm sure would like to meet you," Millie said. "They are good and godly people, and I believe you would have much in common with one of them at least."

"It couldn't do any harm to meet them," Mrs. Sauer said as she was called away by another guest. Millie returned to her room. Charles and Otis had not returned, so she took out her prayer journal and added Mrs. Sauer's name.

The words came back to Millie as she was closing the book: *Cherish each day. You can't imagine you can keep anyone forever.*

A shadow moved across the room as if a cloud had suddenly blocked the sun, and Millie stepped to the window. Charles and Otis were just stepping out of a cab, but the sun shone as brightly as ever. Millie shivered as Charles disappeared beneath the awning. *Cherish each day.* Was the Holy Spirit warning her, as He had warned Paul that he would be killed in Rome? Of course not! Charles is not going to…die. Millie shook the idea from her head and ran down the three flights of stairs to meet her husband.

"We've got a ship!" Charles said, catching her in his arms. "She's not as large as the *Annabelle Lee*, but Mrs. Landreth…we are going to Bolivia!"

"I've got one thing to do before we go," Millie said. "I must invite the Colonel here for tea."

A Piece of Wood

Captain Albright seemed to Millie to be a bright, efficient young man, but strangely irritated from the moment she stepped aboard *The Wanderer*. She was watching the loading of the last of the cargo when he turned to her. "The men need room to work here, and we are in a hurry, Miss. You will have to say your good-byes on the dock."

"She's not saying good-bye," Otis said. "She's a passenger."

"I beg your pardon?" He glanced at the paper in his hand. "The company list said three passengers. Nothing about a woman. Are you man and wife?"

"We are," Charles said, taking Millie's hand.

"I was going to stow all of you in my cabin, but clearly that will not work. You," he pointed to Otis, "you will bunk with the crew. I am sorry for it, but we are a cargo ship and not equipped for passengers."

"I'm sorry to cause you any hardship," Millie said.

The first mate, a grizzled, grumpy-looking sort, gave a short, rasping laugh. "Hardship? Missus, we're horners!"

"Horners?"

"Only the best seamen in the world sail 'round the Horn," the captain said, "but if we make it, you will have sailed the most dangerous waters in the world."

"If? That is not a comforting word, sir," Otis said.

"There is very little comfort to be had on this ship," the captain replied. "But what little we have, we offer the lady," he bowed to Millie. "Mr. and Mrs. Landreth will have my cabin."

"Mil-leeeee!" The voice floated over the harbor sounds, and Millie turned to search the dock.

"There!" Charles pointed.

Colonel Peabody and Mrs. Sauer were waving their caps furiously as they sped past on their running machines.

Millie's Reluctant Sacrifice

Millie laughed as she waved back. Sailors and dockworkers dodged and shook their fists as the two raced away.

"They seem a bit old to be riding those things," Otis said. "I'm sure they are not safe."

The cabin was small but tidy with a round portal window above the bed, a chart table, and a large glass tube, filled with liquid and capped with brass.

"The charts and storm glass will have to stay," Captain Albright said. "And I will have to come in to use them from time to time, but it will be private enough aside from that."

Otis's berth was a shelf against the ship's hull with no room at all for his trunks, which were stowed with the cargo. He was left with two sets of clothing that he kept in a bag at the foot of his bed. He rose greatly in Millie's estimation by not complaining or seeming to mind. *Perhaps Charles is right, Lord, and there is more to Otis Lochneer than meets the eye.*

They dined the night before they sailed at the captain's table, which was in a corner of the galley. There they joined the captain and the first mate, whose name was Chisolm, the five of them making a very cozy company. The food, like everything else on *The Wanderer*, was plain and sufficient. It was served by a cheerful old man with a limp, who was introduced as Theophilus Post.

"That's my name," the old man said with a wink. "But I'll answer to Most Excellent." Otis looked blank, but Millie laughed.

"The physician Luke wrote his Gospel and the book of Acts to the 'most excellent Theophilus,'" she explained. "It means lover of God."

142

A Piece of Wood

"God must love him back," Chisolm said. "The Almighty gave him a toe that tells the weather. When the weatherglass and the toe agree…"

"We'll hope for good weather," Captain Albright said.

"Is rounding Cape Horn truly that dangerous?" Otis asked.

"Yes," the captain said simply. "I've done it six times. The first time was in '34 on a ship called *The Beagle* under the command of Captain Robert FitzRoy."

"But I have his book!" Millie said. "I've brought it with me — *The Commander's Account of a Naval Exploration*, by Captain Robert FitzRoy! The fingerprints of God! He knew we would be here, even on this ship."

Captain Albright nodded. "We will be using FitzRoy's charts. They are the best ever made. He is a meticulous man.

Charles and Millie stood arm in arm the next morning as *The Wanderer* was towed out into the open sea. The tugs released the lines, steaming out of the way. Captain Albright barked orders, and white sails bloomed from the ship's masts. There was a fair wind, and the shore disappeared quickly behind them. They watched until it was out of sight, and then turned to Otis, who was pacing the deck, his hands clasped behind his back, a frown furrowing his brow.

"What are you doing?" Charles asked him at last, when it seemed as though his boots would wear a rut in the deck.

"Anticipating," Otis said. "I am anticipating every single horrible thing that can happen on such a voyage. I have found if I prepare myself for the worst, anything less is a pleasant surprise."

"A woman and a madman," Chisolm muttered under his breath. "Heaven help us!" He stalked away.

"Do you know, Mr. Landreth, that you look uncomfortably like your great-grandfather the privateer as you stand there?" Millie asked.

"Do I?" Charles laughed. "Perhaps his blood does run in my veins. But every last drop of it belongs to Jesus."

Within the week the travelers had learned the rhythms of the ship, the dance of the changing of the watch, the pattern of the days and nights, and Millie knew she was in trouble. There was simply nothing for a lady to do on board; reading her Bible or FitzRoy's journals could take up only so much of the day, and she had sixty such days to look forward to.

She decided at last that if she could not assist the sailors with their duties, she would at least learn navigation and weather science. At the first opportunity, she asked Captain Albright about the storm glass.

"The liquid is a mixture of camphor, ammonia, alcohol, potassium nitrate, and water," the captain explained. "It reacts to invisible changes in the atmosphere, giving us warnings of storms or weather in which the ship might be becalmed.

"If the liquid is clear, as it is now, we will have fine weather. Crystals at the bottom mean frost. If it's cloudy, then we will have rain. Cloudy with crystals means rain with thunder and lightning, large crystals mean snow.

A Piece of Wood

Chains of crystals across the top mean windy weather. If the liquid lies to one side, it means a storm is coming from the other direction."

Millie took note of the condition of the weatherglass each morning, and found it remarkably accurate. Twice, when the liquid was cloudy with crystals, she heard Captain Albright ask Theophilus about the weather.

"Won't be much," the old cook said both times, and both times he was right. They had lightning and rain, but the squall was soon over.

Charles suggested that they hold their evening Bible study in the galley where there was more room. Theophilus loved to listen as he puttered about preparing stew or bread. Otis soon made it a habit to attend—out of sheer boredom, Millie supposed, as he liked to mock and make light of the text.

"Is your uncle a religious man?" Millie asked Otis one day.

"The church has never gained a hold in Bolivia," Otis said. "At least not among the educated class. My uncle is tolerant of those peasants who have religious beliefs, however. He wouldn't dream of interfering with another man's religion."

"What will you do, Otis," she asked, "when you find that believing in God is not just a religion, but that He is real?"

"I will make a deal with Him," Otis said. "This seems to be the way that it is done. I will go to His house on Sundays and sing a few songs to Him, and He, if He is kind and good, will let me into Heaven."

Millie folded her arms. "What if He wants more than weekly visits?" she asked. "Or do you expect that He will scoop you out of Hell for two hours a week in order for you to sing Him a few songs? He doesn't want a visit. He wants your whole life!"

"I have been to church my whole life," Otis said, covering a yawn with his be-ringed fingers. "Forgive me. The Cross is just a piece of wood. But if it makes you feel better to believe something different, my cynicism should not stop you."

"That 'piece of wood' is all that stands between you and death!" Millie felt her temper rising, but Charles gave her a look, and a tiny shake of the head.

"It's not the wood but what happened on it that is important," Charles said. "Until I understood that the Son of God died there in my place, until I let Him take my sins to that Cross, I couldn't come into His presence and know Him."

"I don't think I am contributing to your study," Otis said. "And so I will say good night."

Theophilus glared at his back as he left, slapping a fish onto the chopping block. " 'For the message of the cross is foolishness to those who are perishing.' " *Whack!* The fish head spun across the room. " 'But to us who are being saved it is the power of God!' "

"That's just it. He is perishing, and doesn't even know it." The pain in Charles's voice cut Millie to the heart, and she spent the rest of the evening in repentant prayer.

Millie began to miss her piano the first week of the voyage, and contented herself with playing music in her head. By the third week she was playing scales on a pretend keyboard on the rail. *Please let the Raels have a piano, Lord*, she prayed. *It's hard to think without one.*

As the ship passed into warmer waters, Charles called her on deck one night to see a strange blue-green luminescence in the water. The ship parted it, leaving an ink-black trail behind them.

A Piece of Wood

"Plants in the water," Captain Albright explained. "They glow with their own light."

Millie's journal soon filled with such things—a visitation of pelicans or whales, a flying fish that landed on the deck. Occasionally the ship made port along the way, stopping for fresh kegs of water, vegetables, fruit, and meat. It was a relief to hear a stranger's voice or see a new face. Strangest of all was watching the stars change as they raced south. The constellations Millie had watched since childhood disappeared, replaced by bright Centaurus and the Southern Cross.

One day, as the ship lay at anchor close to an isolated shore on the southern coast of Argentina, Millie tried to find the inlet that sheltered them on her maps, but had no luck.

"Why not name it yourself?" Captain Albright said. "On the voyage of *The Beagle* we named mountains, islands, and inlets. When we reach the coast of Chile, I will show you Mount Darwin. It was named for a young man who was traveling as a naturalist on *The Beagle*. It was his twenty-fifth birthday the day we lay at port there, and Captain FitzRoy named the mountain after him."

Millie took a pencil and, marking the inlet on the map, she wrote *Port Dawn*, because they had watched the sun rise there. She felt as if she were touching creation, the naming of the world, and said as much to Otis.

"But I don't suppose that's the only name it's got," Otis said.

"What do you mean?" Millie looked up from the chart table.

"That mountain in Chile was there long before this chap FitzRoy sailed by, and it must have been called something, by the natives, I mean. It's a bit like a new fellow coming to town and deciding to call me King George, when everyone who knows me calls me Otis, isn't it? Someone must have known that mountain. It's the same with this place, I'd think. Somebody lives here. Or visits at least."

"That's a very good point," Charles said. "I wonder who first named it?" Captain Albright had no answer, as the tribes who lived inland were unknown.

Millie thought about it the next day as they weighed anchor. *Names did not come to the mountains and inlets with the explorers from England, Portugal, or Spain. You did not come with them either, did You, Father?*

It was as if a voice spoke inside her. *"I was here, loving the people who live on that mountain, preparing them for the day they would hear of My Son."* Millie closed her eyes as if she could hear with her heart. *"When He hung on the cross, they were in His heart. He died so that they could be set free. Tell them."*

Millie found herself praying out loud, echoing the words of Paul, "Lord, whenever I open my mouth, may words be given me so that I will fearlessly make known the mystery of the Gospel!"

The world came back with a rush, and Millie found herself gripping the rail, shaken to the core. Had she seen a vision? She hurried to the cabin and wrote the words in her journal, marking the Scripture passage in Ephesians as well. She didn't tell Charles about it until she had awoken three days straight with the same words whispered in her heart again: *"Tell them."*

Charles put his arm around her. "We will tell them together," he said.

And still they sailed south, toward the bottom of the world. Occasionally they sighted albatrosses and giant sea

turtles. Now and again small islands protruded from the waves. Otis suggested that they take the dinghy and row to one of them, but Captain Albright laughed.

"Can't you smell that place?" There was something fetid on the breeze. "It's ankle-deep in seabird guano. I wouldn't want you stepping on my deck after you strolled around that island."

The air became frosty at night, and the sea changed to an angry grey capped with white. Farther on, chunks of ice floated by, the larger ones serving as rafts to strange little black and white birds.

"Penguins," Millie said. "They are penguins! They look like little preachers!"

"I think they look like waiters," Otis said. "And I wish they were serving crumpets and tea."

The ship was two days from the Horn by Captain Albright's reckoning when Millie woke in the morning to find the liquid in the storm glass murky with crystals. "I don't need the glass to tell me a storm is coming," Chisolm said. "I can smell it churning the sea."

The captain consulted with Theophilus and he said the same. A storm coming and a big one; the old man could hardly hobble for the ache in his toe.

"Can we make the Horn?" Charles asked.

"No chance of that," Albright said. "And we can't anchor near the shore. We would be dashed on the rocks. We are going to run into the storm."

The bow of *The Wanderer* was turned away from the shore, and they tacked into the wind. For a day and a half they spent most of their time reading in the cabin, but when Millie could stand it no more, she talked Charles into going to see Captain Albright.

Millie's Reluctant Sacrifice

"We'd like to stay on deck," Charles said, "until the storm breaks."

"Impossible," the captain said. "I could not guarantee your safety."

"If the ship sinks, we shall be quite as drowned beneath decks," Millie pointed out. "And doubtless seasick before we expire."

"You will have to wear lines," the captain said when he finally agreed. "I won't have passengers washed over-board."

For Millie it was exhilarating to watch the wild sea, the swells rising higher and higher as the afternoon progressed. Charles did not feel the same way, but he refused to leave his wife's side. "I never would have dreamed marriage would be so exciting," Charles said with a slightly nervous sigh.

"We've got to face the waves," Captain Albright explained. "If they catch us sideways, the ship will capsize."

Their noonday meal was cold, as it was too rough to build a fire in the galley. After they had eaten, Millie and Charles returned to the deck to watch the dark horizon. Millie had just decided to go back inside when she turned to see the sea rising up in a monstrous swell, higher and higher.

"Get below deck!" Captain Albright yelled, fighting to turn the ship's bow into the wave, and then it was upon them, the wash rising to Millie's knees and knocking her off her feet. Millie felt herself tumbling toward the rail, but the line caught her, and then Charles had her hand. *The Wanderer* turned, shuddered, and righted.

Millie was half dragged to the cabin and shoved inside. They found Otis already there, clinging to the edge of the table.

A Piece of Wood

"Charles!" he said, as Millie gripped the table beside him. "This is worse than my worst imaginings!"

It was impossible to keep one's footing, and everything not tied or nailed down was being thrown from one side of the cabin to the other. They could not hold themselves in place forever. The roar of the storm and the groaning of the ship being battered by the waves was so loud that they could hardly hear one another.

"Let's sit between the table and the bed," Millie yelled. "We can wedge ourselves in." Millie found herself separated from Charles by Otis's pudgy girth, but she was thankful for it nonetheless, for with Otis squeezed between them they were wedged tightly enough not to slide from side to side.

Charles's hand reached for her across Otis, and she took it in her own. It was as dark as if they had been swallowed by a whale—a whale that tossed and pitched and rolled endlessly. *Have the sailors all washed overboard? Is Captain Albright still lashed to the wheel?* wondered Millie.

Charles let go of her hand. He must have reached up and pulled the blanket from the bed, for Millie felt it thrown over her. She tucked it in and closed her eyes against the terrible darkness.

Otis was shaking, and Millie prayed for him and for the ship. She knew Charles must be praying too. Suddenly, Otis was shaking even harder. *He's laughing*, Millie realized. *Otis has lost his mind!*

The storm broke with the morning, and as Otis crawled on his hands and knees toward the cabin door, Charles helped Millie to stand. She was finally able to strip off her wet dress and get into another, but everything in the chest was damp. The ship had sustained some damage in the

storm, enough to make Captain Albright very grim. Theophilus had set a fire in the stove and was cooking a thick pot of porridge for the men, who had been up all night and were working still. Millie sat very near the cookstove.

Otis came in, walking now, scrubbed and clean, his cherub face glowing.

"What could you possibly be cheerful about?" Chisolm growled.

"Last night, for the first time, I realized that nothing stood between me and the darkness but a piece of wood!" he said.

CHAPTER

11

Unfriendly Land?

I will lead the blind by ways they have not known, along unfamiliar paths I will guide them; I will turn the darkness into light before them and make the rough places smooth. These are the things I will do; I will not forsake them.

ISAIAH 42:16

Unfriendly Land?

When you say a piece of wood," Millie said slowly, "do you mean the ship?"

"I mean," Otis said with a twinkle in his eye, "the Cross."

Charles jumped up and shook his friend's hand. "I...I don't know what to say! I have been praying for you for so many years! What—how?"

"I'm not ashamed to say that I was utterly and completely terrified last night," Otis said, sitting down by the stove. "And in my terror, I saw myself clearly for the first time. A little worm of a man, tossed through a storm on a chip of wood, beyond the help of money or influential friends. Just Otis Lochneer. I cried out to God and suddenly I was not alone. There was Someone with me who was mightier than the storm—the same God I had mocked and ignored. I asked Him to forgive me for everything. I knew I wasn't worth one drop of the blood He had shed for me—not one drop. But somehow I knew that He forgave me. He died to save me. It filled me with unspeakable joy!"

"That's why you were laughing last night," Millie said. "I thought you had lost your senses!"

"Rather, I had come to them at last!" Otis said. "And I intend from this day forward to live as the most sensible of men, completely devoted to the work of God." Otis sat down, seeming to have run out of breath and courage all at once. "Now, if I just knew exactly what that was..."

"That's not so hard." Theophilus handed him a bowl of hot gruel. "Says right in the Bible: The work of God is to believe in the One He sent."

Millie's Reluctant Sacrifice

Otis borrowed Charles's Bible and set about God's work that morning, sitting on a water barrel and believing in Jesus with all his heart, as the repair of the ship went on around him.

The Wanderer had lost some sail and snapped some lines; a cargo box that had been secured on the deck had come loose, leaving a splintered, broken rail where it had left the ship for the sea. Millie shuddered to think what might have happened if the crates in the hold had come loose and smashed a hole in the hull. The ropes and cargo nets had held, however, and Charles's precious bottles and vials, which had been packed in straw, seemed to have survived.

Repairs were made while under full sail, and three days later they rounded the Horn under bright blue skies, with brisk, icy winds. Otis had devoted his days to praying, and at night he sat in the warm cabin reading the Bible while Charles pored over medical journals and Millie studied maps and charts.

"Listen to this," Otis said one night. " 'Consequently, faith comes from hearing the message, and the message is heard through the word of Christ.' Charles, do you realize that most of the men on this ship cannot read?"

"Many people cannot," Charles said, looking up from his journal.

"I have never known anyone who could not read before," Otis flushed. "Other than slaves, of course, and they are not allowed. It has occurred to me that I would not have known how to pray, or even who to pray to, if I had not spent years in church. God was planting His Word in me, even if I did not believe it. If these men do not read, and they do not go to church, how do they hear the Word of God?"

"That's a very good question," Charles said.

Unfriendly Land?

"I am determined they will have heard it, as many as want to at any rate, before Otis Lochneer leaves the ship!" He blushed pink. "I may not be able to do much, but I can read. I will read for God."

The next morning Otis began reading the first chapter of Genesis with an audience of three — Theophilus, Charles, and Millie. He had an excellent reading voice and a sense of the dramatic. It was like listening to a monologue or a theatrical production. Otis read for two hours; by the end of the session, his audience had grown by six sailors who had spent the night on duty. He read the same chapters again that evening for those who worked during the day.

Otis was racing the ship, determined to read the entire Bible to the sailors before they reached port.

Millie followed the charts and maps eagerly now, as each day carried them closer to Arica in Chile, where they would leave the ship and continue by mule train.

They had passed the port of Mejillones and were tacking into a stiff wind when a sound like a rifle shot startled the gulls from their perch on the yardarm. Sailors scrambled up the rigging as Mr. Chisolm shouted orders, dropping sail as quickly as they could. The lines of the topsail were cut to free it more quickly, and as it fell, Millie saw the source of the problem — the mast had split. A long, thin crack ran up from the base higher than a man could reach. It was wide enough for her to fit her little finger into, but apparently did not go through the entire mast.

"Never seen anything like it," Chisolm grumbled. "I told you it was bad luck to have a female on board!"

"Nonsense," Captain Albright said. "It must have been damaged in the storm. You might as easily say that Mrs. Landreth has brought us good luck. Why, it could have split completely during the storm and we would have been lost at sea."

A rope was brought and the mast was wrapped for the entire length of the split, as if the mast were a giant spool and the rope the thread. When the rope had been tied off and tightened by means of twisting a belaying pin in it, Captain Albright ordered quarter sail, and they held their breath as the white canvas caught the wind. The mast creaked but held, and they limped slowly up the coast under quarter sail, not daring to leave sight of land lest it split completely and leave them dead in the water.

There was no question now that Otis would finish his mission, and at least twelve seamen heard Genesis 1:1 to Revelations 22:21 before *The Wanderer* made port. He seemed a little disappointed that none of them professed a saving faith in Christ by the end of his reading.

"You were faithful to read," Millie told him as they watched the crates and trunks being carried down the gangplank by the very men he had hoped to save. "Now you must leave the rest up to the Holy Spirit."

Arica was a small port town of mud and stone houses, set between the sea and the dry brown mountains. Otis assured them that his uncle's agent would meet them, and sure enough a grim-faced man met them at the dock. He greeted them in English, introduced himself as Señor Torrez, and assured them that all accommodations had been made for their journey.

"Do you think he has some grudge against doctors?" Charles asked as the man walked away.

"Or perhaps people from the United States," Millie said. *Whatever disease Señor Torrez is afflicted with, it seems to have affected his men as well*, Millie thought, as she, Charles, and

Unfriendly Land?

Otis stood huddled together on the dock while the unloading was done and Captain Albright received his pay.

"That's a grim character you are traveling with," the captain said when he came to bid them good-bye. "You would think someone would have to know you to dislike you that intently. We are going to be in port for at least a month waiting for a new mast, in case you need to return."

This did not comfort Millie at all. *Have we come to an unfriendly land, Lord? What have we done to offend him?* Señor Torrez answered any question Charles or Otis asked of him, but that was all—just the answer.

When the unloading was complete he escorted them to a small inn run by a sturdy woman named Lupe and her daughter Pepita. The long, low building had thick walls made of mud bricks, windows of thick, wavy glass, and bright woven blankets hanging on the walls. Millie stopped to examine a niche which held a soapstone statue of a woman with a thin face who seemed to be carrying a child and several animals on her back, but Lupe pulled her away, ushering her toward her room.

Though Lupe and her daughter spoke no English they were fluent in smiling, and Millie could smile back. They examined her golden hair, asking questions she could not understand, and started to unpack her trunks so the clothes that had been in the damp sea air for so long could dry. When Lupe found a spot of mildew on a pair of pantalets, she pursed her lips, looking so much like Marcia that Millie felt at home and homesick all at once.

The travelers stayed for two days in Arica, long enough for their clothes to dry completely and be repacked. Lupe gave Millie a package of sweet breads and a kiss as the last of the trunks was secured on the mules.

"Why has she been so kind to me?" Millie asked.

Millie's Reluctant Sacrifice

"She believes that if she cares for other people's children, someone will care for hers if they are ever far away," Señor Torrez explained. The man's mood seemed much improved now that they were on their way.

"You can tell her that if her daughter is ever in Pleasant Plains, Indiana, she certainly shall be," Millie said, as Charles lifted her into the saddle. Her horse was too large to be considered a pony, but shaggy and sturdy of leg, and seemed eager enough to travel as they started toward the mountains.

The land was barren, brown, and dry. The small creatures Millie had delighted to watch in Indiana—the squirrels, raccoons, and muskrats—were nowhere to be seen. There were even fewer birds, although these became more abundant as the ground rose into the mountains. Here and there were patches of greenish brown, where grass of a sort was growing, and on these areas they often saw shepherds watching over sheep and llama, long-legged creatures with sweet faces, lovely eyes, and hair softer than the finest wool. Millie thought at first that llama had bright red ears, but soon realized that the creatures' ears were decorated with tassels. Some wore necklaces of bells, gourds, and beads as well.

They camped that first night in a pass high above the sea, under stars brighter than Millie had ever seen before. It was very cold, even in their tents, and they huddled under blankets made of llama wool.

The next morning while Charlie and Otis assisted in breaking camp, Millie set about trying to make friends with the cook by helping where she could, and asking questions by pointing and saying "What is it called?" She soon found that the cook did not want her help, and would not answer, but Señor Torrez would if he heard her question. For instance, he said that the nutty-flavored porridge the cook served them was made from the roasted seeds of a weed-like plant called *quinoa*.

The next day when she saw barefooted women and children stepping on what appeared to be sliced potatoes strewn on rocky ground, she asked Señor Torrez about it. "They are making *chuno*," he said. "They leave the potatoes out to freeze at night. The next day, they press the water out of them with their feet. They continue this for several days until the potatoes are dried. They will keep for a long time, and then they can boil them into a soup."

"That's very clever," Millie said, and she tried to keep that in mind when the cook served them potato soup that evening. "Chuno?" she asked, pointing to it. This time he smiled and nodded. Millie smiled back, trying not to think about sliced potatoes sticking to bare, dirty feet.

"Are you going to finish that soup?" Otis asked. "If not, I will." He patted his stomach. "There's nothing like local cuisine to give you a taste of a new country!"

"It may have a bit too much of Bolivia in it for my taste," Millie said, handing him the bowl. She glanced up to see that the cook was not smiling at her any longer.

Millie explained her lost appetite to Charles, but he only laughed. "It doesn't seem to have done the people here any harm," he said. "And I am sure we eat things that would surprise them as well."

That evening, Millie prayed over her soup and ate every bite. The cook did not seem to have forgiven her, though.

"I feel more isolated than I did on the ship," Charles said as he rode beside her on the third day. "At least the sailors spoke to us."

Millie's Reluctant Sacrifice

"Do you think Señor Torrez has told them not to talk with us for some reason?"

"I don't know," Charles said. "I hope Otis's uncle gives us a warmer greeting."

Millie was thoroughly tired of mules, saddles, and camping fourteen days later when they finally reached La Paz, a huge city of glittering cathedrals, markets, and crowded, noisy streets. She was delighted to learn they would have hot baths and clean sheets for two whole nights, as Señor Torrez had business to attend to in the city. He hired a small boy named Philipe to guide Millie, Charles, and Otis while he was occupied, and left them on their own.

That night they ate at a street cafe, and listened to music from a ten-stringed instrument made from an armadillo shell. "*Charango*," Philipe said when Millie pointed at it.

They dined on boiled potatoes and chicken seasoned with robust herbs, a plate of thickly sliced goat, vegetables in cream sauce, and a cup of thick mango juice, which Millie found delicious. For dessert they had fried plantains, which were like firm bananas.

"I love this country!" Otis said when they were done, although it was not clear how much the good meal had contributed to his statement.

Philipe squatted by the front entrance of the hotel, waiting for them to appear the next morning. Millie suspected that he slept in the doorway. The first place he took them to on their tour was an eatery to purchase breakfast. He wolfed down the plate of food that was put before him, and then pointed to the street.

"All right," Charles said. "Lead on!" The streets were full of peasants selling goods or bartering for what they needed, and they examined the foreigners, especially Millie, with interest. Philipe strutted as if these new, strange creatures were his own property, showing them off to shopkeepers and farmers alike.

"Have you noticed," Charles asked as the day wore on, "that La Paz seems to be made exclusively of shops selling sweets?"

"You don't suppose our guide could be biased in favor of bakeries, do you?" Millie pretended shock.

"I do suppose it," Charles said. "In fact, I believe we had been in that last establishment before, say, two hours ago."

Philipe was dancing ahead of them, his pockets bulging with sweets that "Tio Otees" had bought him.

"Philipe," Millie called. "We don't want to go that way. We are going to turn down this street."

"No," the little boy said, running back and taking her hand.

"Yes," Millie laughed. "What's the matter? Are there no candy shops down this street?"

"No!" Philipe pulled her hand. "Es un calle malo! Malo!"

He gave up when Millie and Charles started down the street anyway, following close behind them.

"I think I prefer bakeries," Otis said, as the street seemed to narrow to an alley.

The vendors did not call out to them, but watched them with glittering eyes from booths filled with jars and powders, dried plants, and small statues.

"What is this place?" Charles asked. He stepped closer to a stall, touching a yellow powder in a bowl. "Sulfur," he decided. The bowl next to it held iron powder; others were unidentifiable, as were tiny glass bottles of murky liquids. "It's like a chemist's shop."

Millie's Reluctant Sacrifice

"Look at these odd dolls," Otis said, pointing to a basket full of strange brown creatures with tangled hair and huge, sunken eyes.

"Those are not dolls." They all jumped at the sound of Señor Torrez's voice. Philipe grabbed Millie's skirts as if to hide in the folds of fabric. "They are…what is the word?…baby llamas."

"They're dried fetuses," Charles said. Millie took a step back. "Born too soon to survive, I think. What is this place?" he asked.

"Laki'asina Catu," Señor Torrez said. "The witches' market. We should be getting back to the hotel now." He spoke to Philipe in Spanish, and the little boy cringed.

"He's done a good job," Millie said, putting her arm around the boy. "He tried to keep us from coming here, but I insisted."

"He was wise, then. This is no place for you." He started walking, and they had to hurry to keep up.

"Why would they sell dead llamas?" Otis asked. "What good are they?"

"A great deal of good if you worship Pachamama. They are offered to her in sacrifice, when a family is too poor to give a live llama," replied Señor Torrez.

"Who is Pachamama?" Otis asked.

"The little statues are of Pachamama," Señor Torrez said, pointing. "The child on her back is her daughter, the goddess Mama Coca. The creatures are her helpers. A statue of Pachamama brings her protection to a home."

Like the one at the inn where we first stayed, Millie thought. *I must remember to pray for Lupe and Pepita*. Millie resisted the urge to look over her shoulder several times, refusing to give in to the feeling that something was following her out of that dark place.

Unfriendly Land?

Otis sat with them in their room that night, seeming hesitant to leave. Charles seemed troubled as well, flipping through his Bible, reading a passage, then finding another, a wrinkle between his brows. "I can't help but think about what your Aunt Wealthy said about demons," he said. "And I cannot reconcile it with what Dr. Fox taught me—demons were illnesses such as seizures of the brain."

"I have never heard of a seizure of the brain leaping from a human to a pig," Otis pointed out. "But that clearly happened in the eighth chapter of Luke."

Millie laughed. "I can't believe you are the same Otis Lochneer who believed that demons were just—how did you phrase it—'the product of a medieval mind'!"

"I had never read the Bible for myself," Otis said. "Now that I have, I must admit that Jesus believed in them. And if He believed, then I must also."

"I am not sure I can escape it, even though I want to," Charles said. "What else did Wealthy say? That you couldn't march into a land in spiritual darkness and announce freedom to the captives without those spirits noticing?"

"I have the feeling we have been noticed," Otis said.

"Pish-tosh," Millie said, refusing to give in to the shivers that were trying to trickle down her spine. "God would not want His children to be afraid of doing His work, no matter where they are or what they are facing."

"If we are going to accept that demons are real, we can't forget what it says in Ephesians 6:13," Charles said, opening his Bible. "Therefore put on the full armor of God, so that when the day of evil comes, you may be able to stand your ground, and after you have done everything, to stand. Stand firm then, with the belt of truth buckled around your waist, with the breastplate of righteousness in place, and with your feet fitted with the readiness that comes from the gospel of peace."

"The truth is that Jesus has won the battle," Millie said. "And His righteousness protects our hearts."

"In addition to all this," Charles continued reading, "take up the shield of faith, with which you can extinguish all the flaming arrows of the evil one. Take the helmet of salvation, and the sword of the Spirit, which is the word of God. And pray in the Spirit on all occasions with all kinds of prayers and requests." This last they proceeded to do for an hour, and peace settled over Millie as they prayed.

"I feel much better," Otis said, standing up to leave at last. "Only...Charles...May I borrow a sword? You have two." He went to his own room with Charles's Bible tucked under his arm.

"I think we are going to have to buy Bibles by the crate, Mr. Landreth," Millie said with a smile. "You don't seem to be able to keep them."

"That's true," Charles said. "And I doubt we will find an English version in all of Bolivia. Are you afraid, Millie?" he asked suddenly. "Of the darkness in Bolivia?"

"God gave me a Scripture before I married you, Charles Landreth, before I even knew I was coming to Bolivia. He said, 'I will give you treasures hidden in darkness.' I can ask for no greater treasures than the souls of those we are sent to preach to. I hope the Hacienda Rael has a piano. I miss playing hymns each night."

CHAPTER

12

False Prophets and Gods

Now this is eternal life: that they may know you, the only true God, and Jesus Christ, whom you have sent.

JOHN 17:3

False Prophets and Gods

They were back on their horses and an hour out of La Paz before Otis realized that two rings were missing from the hand that Philipe had held so tightly the day before. There was nothing they could do but shake their heads and pray for the boy; there had been no sign of him when they departed. Their trail took them past ancient ruins on the shore of a lake, where husks of buildings made from huge blocks of stone were all that remained of a once mighty civilization.

Awed by the size of the stones, Millie asked Señor Torrez, "Who built these?"

"The old ones," he said. "They were gone long before the Spaniards came."

Millie was more aware now, and noticed that the men with the mule train would occasionally slip aside to leave gifts at a rock or cairn at an overlook or at a mountain pass. When Charles asked Señor Torrez about it, the man explained that they were leaving offerings for the various gods of the mountains and valleys, and seemed to think it was a natural thing to do.

The single-file track left little chance for talking to one another while they were traveling, but afforded hours to pray each day, and Millie spent her time praying for the people of Bolivia and for God to give her the grace to be there. At last they came through a mountain pass, and a valley, hung on the shoulders of the mountain, stretched before them.

They stopped for the view while Señor Torrez pointed out the town of Orofino, several hundred mud houses surrounded by terraced fields, and the Hacienda of Don Francisco Rael, a distant white dot on a hill.

Millie's Reluctant Sacrifice

"What is that?" Millie asked, pointing to something resembling an anthill, with small figures coming out of a hole, depositing their loads, and returning.

"That is one of Don Rael's mines," Señor Torrez said. "We will pass it on the trail."

"We would like to observe the operation," Charles said. "If it is not inconvenient."

Señor Torrez agreed, sending the men and pack mules on ahead with instructions to prepare for their arrival.

What had appeared to be ants from the height of the pass were humans, drenched in sweat even in the cold air, and straining under the heavy loads of ore they carried in bags on their backs.

Charles helped Millie from her saddle, and they walked to the edge of the pit. She grabbed his hand at the sudden feeling of vertigo as she looked into the pit. A line of half-naked men was ascending by way of notched poles, which zigzagged across the shaft.

"How much are they carrying?" Otis asked.

"These are good men," Señor Torrez said. "Each load will weigh close to two hundred pounds. Each man carries twenty-four hundred pounds—twelve loads—of ore a day."

"How is that possible?" Millie asked.

"They are Quechua," Señor Torrez shrugged, as if this explained it. "They chew the coca leaf."

A miner, as if knowing what they were talking about, spat a wad of something into the dirt. He fished several green leaves from a belt at his pouch, tucked them into his mouth, and chewed vigorously. A bulge appeared in his cheek as he wadded the leaves there. He smiled widely at Millie, showing horribly decayed teeth as he fished in a

second pouch for a pinch of white powder, which he apparently added to the leaves.

"Lye," Torrez explained. "It draws the juice from the leaves."

"And these leaves help them work?" Charles asked.

"They could not stand the cold of the mines without the coca," Señor Torrez said. "It keeps them warm and gives them strength. Keeps them alive."

The Hacienda of Don Rael was indeed a palace, far richer than any mansion Millie had seen in the South. They passed through iron gates onto a long drive, with expansive gardens on either side, though the vegetation was strange to Millie's eyes.

A regal man stood on the wide steps, awaiting them. He had gold braids on his pants and his jacket, and was dressed much too richly for a servant, Millie was sure. Her suspicions were confirmed when Otis jumped from the saddle.

"Uncle Francisco! Aunt Angela!" he called, bounding up the stairs. "I told you I would bring a doctor, and here he is!" He waved grandly at Charles. "Charles Landreth, M.D."

"Francisco Rael, at your service," Don said. "I am delighted that you have come, and I welcome you and your wife into my home." Servants held the massive doors as they stepped inside.

It was as if they had stepped from Bolivia, with its mud houses and peasants, through a doorway to Spain. The entry hall was rich with Persian rugs and carved mahogany woodwork. Millie was sure the king of Spain himself would

feel at home in this place. But it was the woman at the end of the hall that drew Millie's attention.

"Hello, Otis! It's good to see my favorite nephew again," said Angela.

"May I present Doña Angelina Rael?" Don Rael said to Charles and Millie, who could hear the love in his voice.

"Call me Angela, please!" Angela Rael was too thin to be beautiful, but it was forgotten as soon as you looked into her eyes. They were blue-green lamps of joy, shining out of her soul. An elderly woman stood beside her, a protective hand on her arm.

"I would add to my husband's welcome!" Angela said, reaching out a hand. Millie realized for the first time that the woman was in a wheelchair, and stepped forward to take her hand. "I am so delighted that we can offer you hospitality." The soft tones of the South still colored her speech. "You cannot imagine how I have longed for a woman's company. Now, Aida," she put a hand on the arm of the old woman at her side. "I don't mean to hurt your feelings. I meant only someone from home. And may I present my daughter, Savannah?"

A woman with the stiff look of a governess pushed a little girl of eight or nine forward. The child had her mother's fine features and her father's dark coloring, and she was dressed in riches of laces, satin, and brocades. Savannah made a very proper curtsey, but did not say a word.

"And this is Señorita Armijo," Don Rael said, as the governess inclined her head. "A very important part of our household. You will find her English excellent and her manners beyond reproach."

"I am —" Angela Rael bent forward in a cough, holding a white handkerchief to her lips.

"You must not tire yourself," Don Rael said, moving quickly to his wife's side. "Let Aida take you to your room, and you will be rested for dinner."

"I believe you are right." She hid the kerchief quickly, but Millie was sure she had seen blood on it. She glanced at Charles. He had seen it as well, and his face was grim.

Angela gave them an apologetic smile. "I look forward to seeing you then." Her servant wheeled her away.

Don Rael spoke to Señor Torrez briefly in Spanish and then dismissed him before leading Charles, Otis, and Millie to his study, a vast room that seemed to double as a library. The walls were lined with shelves of books, most in Spanish and some in English.

"You have come none too soon," he said. "My Angie…is worse today, and has been very ill for the last month. She is my life, doctor. This," he waved his arm at the richness of the room, as if to brush it away like cobwebs, "means nothing to me now. Make her well, Dr. Landreth, and I will make you a wealthy man."

"Your wife is gravely ill," Charles said. "I believe there was blood on her handkerchief."

"Yes," Don Rael said. "I am not a fool or a dreamer. But I refuse to lose hope."

"Might I examine her now?" Charles asked, but Don Rael shook his head.

"There will be time after we dine. She is resting now. We have been anxious about your arrival since the runner came with news that you were in the valley."

A flash of white caught Millie's eyes—Savannah's pale face, almost hidden in the shadows. The little girl stood as still as a fawn, listening to every word they said. Millie turned away, pretending that she hadn't seen.

Millie's Reluctant Sacrifice

"But tell me of your journey. You are from Chicago, I understand?"

"I lived in Chicago for several years," Charles said, "but traveled to Indiana to marry my wife."

"Ah," Don Rael smiled and shook his head. "I traveled to Charleston, South Carolina, to find mine." He turned to Otis. "And you are not married yet?"

"Not yet, Uncle," Otis said.

Don Rael studied him. "You have changed."

"Agreeably so, I hope," Otis said. "It has been quite a journey from New York."

"You will have to tell me more at dinner," Don Rael said. "Now, I believe the lady might like to freshen up." A servant appeared out of nowhere. "Roberto will show you to your rooms, and you will be summoned for dinner."

They thanked him and followed Roberto down the halls, their feet silent on the thick carpet. The Landreths were given a suite of rooms that would have been sufficient for a family of six.

"I must find out where they have put my medical supplies," Charles said, after examining the trunks that had been delivered to their rooms. "I see no reason I cannot have them here, and I need some of my journals." He went in search of Roberto.

"We're here, Lord!" Millie said, spreading her arms. "And I am ready for the treasures You promised!"

"Are you a bruja?"

Millie turned to find Savannah looking at her. "What is a bruja?"

"A witch."

"Certainly not!" Millie said.

"My father said that healers were coming. Brujas can heal."

"Magic cannot save lives, Savannah," Millie said. "Only God can do that."

Savannah's dark eyes examined her, and Millie felt as if she were being weighed and found wanting, or ignorant at the very least. "Wanunu says my mother is sick because her spirit does not belong here."

"Who is Wanunu?"

"She is a powerful bruja," Savannah said. "She says the white man's god is no good in the mountains. Wanunu says he doesn't live here. Tupac says Wanunu is *supaya wawan* — a devil's daughter. "

"And who is Tupac?" Millie asked.

"Tupac is a Quechua boy." Savannah's chin went up. "He thinks that I am a princess. Tupac and Tomas are brothers."

"And why does Tupac say such things about Wanunu?" Millie pronounced the name carefully.

"Because she killed his little sister," Savannah said seriously. "With a night fever."

"Savannah!" Señorita Armijo was in the door. "You are not to pester the young lady with your stories. My apologies, señora. Savannah spends too much time with peasant children."

"She wasn't bothering me at all," Millie said, smiling.

Señorita Armijo sniffed. "It is time to dress for dinner," she said, and Savannah followed her from the room.

Millie told Charles of her conversation with the child as they arranged his books on the shelves. "Do you think that a bruja could make someone sick?" she asked.

He shook his head. "I have a hard time believing it. Still, demons did make people ill in the Bible."

They finished unpacking the books, and then hurriedly dressed for dinner. Millie had just finished twisting her hair into a French knot when a servant arrived to summon them to the dining room.

Angela was seated next to her husband, looking much refreshed after the rest. Señorita Armijo was on her left, her grey hair pulled into a bun so severe that it gave her eyebrows a look of perpetual surprise and disapproval. Savannah, who sat beside her governess, was silent once more, and Millie decided it was the quiet of a sickroom, grown through long habit of being near her mother. The little girl watched everything intently, however, and Millie was sure her brown eyes missed nothing.

"Señor Torrez has given me an account of your journey from Arica," Don Rael said, "but I would like to hear of your travel by ship."

Otis's description of pelicans, penguins, and whales had them all laughing, and when he described the storm, Millie practically felt the wind.

"I am glad you made it safely to port," Señora Rael said. "It would never do to have a cousin washed away on his way to rescue me."

"I would give my life to rescue you, Tia Angie," Otis said seriously.

"You are gallant, señor." Don Rael smiled.

"We grow them that way in the South, Francisco," Angela said. "Cotton, sugar, and fine gentlemen are our chief exports."

"And I'm sure your fine gentlemen are shrewd businessmen as well. Otis will no doubt want to check on his father's investment. Tomorrow we will tour the mines if you like," Don Rael said. "The one you visited is the only shaft from which we do not pump water."

The conversation turned to pumping machines and mine depths. Millie was a little disappointed when she realized

that the invitation included only Charles and Otis, but Señora Rael smiled so hopefully at her that Millie relented at once.

After the meal, Charles again asked if he could examine his patient, and this time permission was granted. Millie stood by while he listened to Angela's heart and lungs, then sat down to ask questions. Her illness had begun over a year ago with a cough, then a sudden weakness of the legs. Charles examined her spine and made more notes. He finally ordered water boiled in her room all night with camphor added to it. She had been urged by one physician to stay in bed, or her chair, until her strength returned, but Charles encouraged her to stand for a few moments twice a day, and swing her arms while she was seated to improve her circulation.

The next morning Charles and Otis rode out with Don Rael. Millie spent the morning in pleasant conversation with Angela while Aida pushed the wheelchair through the rooms of the house. Millie exclaimed in delight when they came upon a music room complete with a grand piano.

"Do you play?" Angela asked, and when Millie admitted that she did, Angela begged for a tune. "A waltz," she said. "I would give anything to waltz again!"

Millie played a waltz, and then another.

"I know you are a guest, and the doctor is working for my husband," Angela said. "But I think music is better than medicine for me!"

"Then you shall have as much as you like," Millie said. "My heart will not be happy without it. I have missed it for months." She played until her fingertips tingled.

They had lunch together, and then Angela covered a yawn. "I am so sorry to be such a poor hostess," she said.

Millie's Reluctant Sacrifice

"But I am afraid I am exhausted, Mrs. Landreth. You must tell your husband for me that I stood for five whole minutes this morning."

"He will be delighted to hear it, I'm sure."

Angela's head was already nodding when Aida pushed her from the room. Millie was glad to have some time to herself to think about the things she had heard and seen. She put on her walking shoes and bonnet and went out through the garden gate. The hill rose steeply behind the house, completely wild and dry. Millie had to rest frequently on the way up, but she found the top at last, and a rock that made a perfect lookout point. The view was all brown mountains and blue sky, as far as she could see, with ribbons and patches of green where there were fields or streams.

The Hacienda was below her, and beyond that, the town. *I wonder if this is what Moses felt like on the mountain? Or David when he watched over his sheep? All alone with God. They both knew that God was watching over them. And He is watching over us as well. What is the truth about brujas, Lord? Have we traveled back into biblical times with false prophets and gods?* Millie spent an hour praying before she made her way back down the mountain.

She played the piano for Angela again after supper that night, and after Don Rael had pushed her wheelchair out of the room, played hymns while Charles and Otis sang.

"Do you like it here?" Charles asked as they walked in the garden one night. The air was cold, and Millie had her wool shawl around her shoulders.

"Yes," she said. "But home feels very far away."

"Let me bring it a little closer," Charles said, putting his arms around her. "Does that help?"

"It does, a little," Millie said.

"Only a little?"

178

"I once thought that Keith Hill was like a puddle of heaven that had spilled onto the earth. I miss it. Did you know that there is no church in Orofino?"

"Then we have come to the right place to start one. Will you attend church this Sunday with me, Mrs. Landreth? We will hold it in the music room. You can play the piano, and I will preach."

"I believe the Rael family might attend," Millie said. "But the peasants will not come inside the Hacienda. You once confessed to me that you had never seen a soul come to Jesus." Millie snuggled closer to him. "Now I will confess to you that I am not sure how to tell the Quechua people about Jesus. I have learned a few words of Spanish, but the Quechua people don't speak it."

"Then we will learn Quechua."

But a month passed without any opportunity to start, and Millie fell into a daily routine of talking with Señora Rael and pushing her through the gardens if the weather was warm, or sitting and talking in the conservatory if it was not. Angela and Savannah were happy to join their visitors for prayer and a Bible lesson on Sunday mornings, but Don Rael would not attend. Their little church grew by two when Angela told Señora Armijo and Aida that she would like their company, but they sat quietly the whole time, their hands folded in their laps.

Thoughts of brujas and Old Testament stories seemed to vanish from Millie's mind as the days went by. The Hacienda was a quiet, peaceful place and Señora Rael was pleasant company. Millie had soon taken over the chore of helping her to stand twice a day, and even take a few steps.

Charles and Don Rael spent hours riding together, and Otis seemed to have acquired a small swarm of children who followed him every time he left the Hacienda grounds or walked the streets of Orofino. Millie suspected that this had something to do with the horehound candy he kept in his pockets, until she came upon them during one of her prayer walks, and found herself watching a drama.

Otis Lochneer was dancing madly around a small pile of rocks, while a group of children, none older than ten, laughed and pointed. One boy had a baby llama, led by a rope. Its long neck was decorated with garlands of flowers and bells; even this creature seemed to be watching Otis in disbelief.

"Whatever are you doing?" Millie asked, trying not to laugh. Otis jumped at the sound of her voice.

"Oh, it's you, Millie," he said, straightening his collar. "I am enacting a Bible story," Otis said. "And Savannah is my translator."

Millie sat down with the children. "You amaze me, Otis," she said. "You have established a Bible school without telling us!"

"Hardly that," Otis blushed. "But they do seem to enjoy the stories."

Something tugged at her bonnet, and Millie grabbed it just before the llama managed to pull it away.

"Pilpintu!" the boy scolded.

"Pilpintu," Millie tickled its chin. "That's a lovely name."

"It means butterfly," Savannah explained. "Because her eyelashes are so long, you see. Her mother died, but Tomas saved her. He gave her to Tupac."

"And is this Tupac?" He was a handsome boy with dark skin, a smile like sunshine, and wild, bushy hair.

"Yes," Savannah said. "Tupac said she is half mine. We gave her milk from our cow, but now she is old enough to eat grass."

"Primo Otis! Primo Otis!" a little girl called. Savannah turned to her with a frown.

"*My* cousin Otis," she said firmly. "Not yours. They want the rest of the story, cousin."

"I do hope you will go on with your theatre," Millie said.

"Of course." Otis cleared his throat. "We were enacting the story of Elijah on Mount Carmel." Suddenly, he threw his arms in the air. "They called on the name of Baal from morning till noon. 'O Baal, answer us!'" He looked out over his audience and shook his head. "But nothing happened. Nothing at all."

Savannah translated this for the children, and Millie had to hide her smile. The little girl copied Otis's dramatic diction and his every motion as well. As the story went on, the circle of children edged closer, fascinated by every word.

When it was Elijah's turn, Otis pretended to pour water over a stone altar—one, two, three, four pitchers; then he prayed, and jumped back as if the stones were on fire.

"'The fire of the Lord fell and burned up the sacrifice, the wood, the stones, and the soil, and also licked up the water in the trench!'"

Savannah translated, but Tupac jumped to his feet, evidently arguing with her.

She folded her arms and looked up at Otis. "He says that fire does not lick up water."

"Ah!" Otis said, nodding his head. "Ah! Tell him that this book," he held up his Bible, "is God's Word. And it is true."

Savannah did this. Tupac sat down, his lips pursed.

Millie's Reluctant Sacrifice

"When all the people saw this, they fell face down," said Otis, demonstrating this action to the great delight of the children, "and cried, 'The Lord—he is God! The Lord—he is God!'"

Savannah threw herself on the ground and cried out in Quechua. The children gasped and looked at one another.

"Savannah!" Tupac called. He pointed to the edge of the clearing. A grim-faced woman was watching them.

"Wanunu," someone whispered.

"Hello," Millie said, as Otis scrambled to his feet. The woman ignored her. She pointed a finger at Savannah and spoke in Quechua. The little girl turned pale and backed toward Otis.

"Now see here," he said, realizing that something wasn't right, but the woman ignored him as well, taking a step closer to Savannah.

Tupac was on his feet in an instant, between the bruja and his princess, his fists clenched at his side. He shouted something at the woman and she stopped. Her eyes narrowed, and she turned and walked away.

"Something very bad is going to happen," Savannah whispered. "Very bad!"

"Pish-tosh," Millie said, brushing the dust from the little girl's dress. "But we had better get you cleaned up before Señorita Armijo sees you."

CHAPTER

13

Time to Stand

*Have I not commanded you? Be strong
and courageous. Do not be terrified;
do not be discouraged, for the
Lord your God will be with
you wherever you go.*

JOSHUA 1:9

Time to Stand

*T*hat woman positively frightens me," Otis said, as they described the encounter to Charles that night. "I wish I knew what she said to Savannah, but the girl wouldn't say."

"Have you spoken to your uncle about it?" Charles asked. "I'm sure he would not allow his daughter to be threatened."

"Uncle Rael does not get involved with the peasants," Otis said. "They are...beneath him."

"That's true," Charles said. "He doesn't even speak to them directly. He gives orders through Señor Torrez. Still, if it concerns his daughter, I'm sure you should speak to him."

Millie decided she would do just that, at the first opportunity. There was something about that old woman Wanunu that gave Millie the same feeling she had experienced in the witches' market in La Paz—ancient and evil.

"I have news that might be of interest to you," Charles said. "We begin work on the clinic tomorrow."

"What!"

"You will love the site," he said. "It has a wonderful view."

"All of Bolivia has a wonderful view," Millie said. "If you like mountains and sky."

"These mountains and this sky are more beautiful than most," he assured her. "Don Rael has offered to pay any men who will help with the building the same as if they were working in the mines."

185

Millie's Reluctant Sacrifice

It was decided that Señor Torrez would accompany them to the site of the new clinic while Don Rael spent the day with his wife, who would be lacking Millie's company. Savannah begged to come with them and Señorita Armijo allowed it.

Millie collected her Bible, in case there were spare hours to read, and a basket lunch, which had been prepared for them, and they mounted their mountain horses.

Millie had to admit it was a beautiful spot, halfway between the mines and the village, with a trickle of dampness on the rock face behind it that hinted at water if they should dig a well. They gathered in the center of the small clearing and bowed their heads in prayer and thanksgiving, while Señor Torrez looked on.

"Do you think many will come?" Otis asked when the prayer was done.

"I think so," Charles laughed and pointed down the road. The entire village seemed to be marching up the path, some men with shovels and picks and others with musical instruments that they played as they walked. The women and children followed behind.

"I think someone declared a picnic!" Millie said.

Señor Torrez gave brief instructions when the workers arrived, and they started digging into the side of the hill where Charles had marked out the corners of the foundation.

The work was progressing surprisingly well for the rocky soil when Señor Torrez called out and the workers stopped.

At first Millie could not tell why they had stopped, and then the crowd around them started to stir and parted. Millie was looking directly into the cold and flinty eyes of

Wanunu. Wanunu walked toward them, leading a beautiful young llama.

"Pilpintu!" Savannah cried. She ran to a Quechua woman and pulled on her hand, obviously asking for her friend Tupac.

Wanunu spoke to the crowd, and they murmured and fell to their knees.

"Wanunu has come to dedicate this house of healing to the goddess Pachamama," Señor Torrez said. "The llama will be sacrificed and buried in the foundation. The building will have the blessing of the goddess of the mountains."

"Otis," Savannah whispered urgently, "she has taken Pilpintu. Tupac is sick and Tomas is away on the mountain!"

"This ground is not dedicated to the goddess," Millie said firmly. "It is dedicated to Jesus, the King of all."

"It is a harmless custom," Señor Torrez said, "allowed by Don Rael. The people have done this for more generations than can be remembered. Even the Hacienda has a llama buried in the foundation."

"Nonetheless," Charles said, stepping closer to Millie. "This clinic is dedicated to Jesus, not to a goddess."

Wanunu did not understand their words, but she could understand the tone of voice. Her eyes narrowed and she stepped forward, pulling the baby llama with her.

"No!" Millie stepped forward. "There will be no sacrifice to Pachamama!"

Otis took the llama's lead from the woman's hand, and the crowd gasped.

"Tell them what I say, Savannah," Millie opened her Bible and began to read. " 'In the beginning was the Word, and the Word was with God, and the Word was God. He was with God in the beginning.' " She waited for the little girl to translate. " 'Through him all things were made; without him nothing was made that has been made. The light shines in the darkness, but the darkness has not understood it.' " Millie closed her Bible, waiting for Savannah to finish. "These mountains were not created by Pachamama. They were created by Jesus," declared Millie.

Wanunu hissed when she heard the name Jesus. At this, a chill ran down Millie's spine and her voice felt like it was quivering, but she went on. "He created the Quechua people. He loves them, and wants them to come to Him and be healed. That is why this house of healing is dedicated to Him. Jesus does not ask for you to sacrifice your llamas to Him. Instead, He gave Himself up as a sacrifice for *you*."

When Savannah finished, the people began to whisper among themselves. Suddenly, Wanunu raised her hand, fingers spread wide, and silence spread from her like ripples across the surface of the crowd. She pulled her hand down, as if she were pulling power from the sky, and began to speak in a deep, rasping voice.

"What is she saying?" Millie asked.

"She is cursing this ground," Señor Torrez said. "She says no healing will occur here. Those who work on this building will be cursed, and they will die."

"Pish-tosh," Millie said, folding her arms.

Wanunu spat, and the spittle hit Millie's face.

"Charles, don't!" Millie said as he started forward. "Just let her go. We have work to do here."

Wanunu settled herself on a rock and seemed to go to sleep. The crowd stood silently now.

"Are they going to go back to work?" Otis asked hopefully.

188

"No," Señor Torrez said. "They are waiting to see how you die."

"My uncle could force them to work," Otis offered.

"I don't think they should be forced to work for Jesus," Charles said. He picked up a shovel and pushed it down hard, filling it with dirt. Millie picked up another.

"Millie Landreth!" Charles said. "Shoveling is hardly a ladylike occupation."

"Nonsense!" Millie said. "I will tell you what is not lady-like. It is not ladylike to allow these people to be ruled by darkness. That would not be ladylike at all, to my way of thinking."

Otis gave the llama's lead rope to Savannah and took up a pick, but Señor Torrez just sat on his horse looking over the crowd, his hand on the butt of his pistol.

"It would be more helpful to put his hand on a shovel," Millie said, after they had been working for about an hour, but it made no difference to Señor Torrez. They worked until the sun was directly overhead, and then they stopped for their picnic—hot, tired, and discouraged. It seemed they had just scratched the surface of the ground, and their shovels had struck rocks at every turn.

"Can you die of blisters?" Otis asked as Millie poured a cup of cool water.

"I wouldn't give her the satisfaction, even if you could," she said, handing it to him. "This woman has these people completely under her thumb."

"I wonder if there is a reason for it?" Charles looked across the clearing to where Señor Torrez still sat like a statue. They bowed their heads and thanked God for the food, and then ate their meal. He didn't offer to join them.

Millie's Reluctant Sacrifice

"I think he is standing guard," Charles said as they stood up to work once more. "Now who is this?"

A young man was running toward them. Not paying any heed to the path, he jumped like a goat from rock to rock, taking the shortest path until he reached them.

"Tomas!" Savannah cried. The young man looked around, taking in the silent crowd, Señor Torrez still unmoving on his horse, and Pilpintu leaning against Savannah.

He walked over to Millie, grabbed her shovel, and tried to pull it away. Millie tried to pull it back, but he wouldn't let go.

"Give him the shovel, Millie," Charles said, sounding slightly stunned.

"But what will I dig with?"

"You won't, Millie. I know this boy. He is the young man from my dream."

Millie let go of her shovel. Tomas dug a mighty shovelful and threw it over his shoulder. Then he raised his shovel in one hand and shouted defiance at the mountain and at Wanunu.

The bruja had come awake, it seemed. She called out something, and Tomas grabbed his shovel and started digging fiercely, as if fighting the mountain itself.

"What did she say?" Millie asked.

"She said he is digging Tupac's grave." Savannah's voice was frightened. "They will put him in it tomorrow. They die at night, Millie. They always do when Wanunu says they will."

"We will be with your friend tonight," Charles promised. "After the sun goes down. Until then, we dig."

Tomas made much better progress against the rocky soil than Millie had, and she contented herself with sitting by

190

Savannah and praying as the outline of a foundation took shape.

"Tomas hates Wanunu," Savannah explained as she petted Pilpintu's nose. "He kills the serpents that are her servants when he catches them in the hills. He says that Pachamama is evil. A good god would not send fevers to kill children. Tomas is brave. He says he will not worship an evil god—not even if she kills him."

Come and help us, Jesus. Millie pleaded. *You heard this young man's prayer, even though he does not know You yet! His heart is crying out for freedom. Speak to him, Lord. He can't understand our language, but he can understand Your Spirit. Show us how to help him!*

Finally, when the shadow of the mountain stretched toward them, Charles put his shovel over his shoulder.

"Savannah," Millie said quietly. "I think you should take Pilpintu home with you until Tupac is better."

"We will go to your brother now," Charles said, though Tomas could not understand. "I will need to stop by the Hacienda and get my bag."

"I will take Savannah home," Señor Torrez offered, "and bring your bag to you, and candles as well. You don't have much time. The sun is sinking."

"Millie, I'm afraid!" Savannah said.

"You just take care of Pilpintu," Millie said. "We will look after Tupac."

Charles gave Señor Torrez instructions on finding the bag and what to bring in it, and asked him to tell Don Rael where they were. Then they started down the trail to Orofino. Wanunu followed them, and the crowd came after her, like a funeral parade.

Millie's Reluctant Sacrifice

Tomas led them to a small mud house with a thatched roof.

The crowd gathered around the house as they went inside. Millie was glad to shut the door, such as it was, behind them.

The dirt floor was swept clean, and the brothers' beds, two mats on the floor, appeared clean as well. In one corner of the room was a small fireplace. Tupac sat at a wooden table, and a rocking chair sat before the fire. He looked up, and Tomas said something to him. Millie caught the names Pilpintu and Savannah, and Tupac smiled.

Tupac rested his elbows on the table, all of the light gone from his brown eyes. His wild hair hung in his face, and his shoulders slumped forward. As Charles went toward him, the little boy looked at his older brother, who nodded encouragement.

"He has only a slight fever, Tomas," Charles said reassuringly after he had examined the child. "It does not seem to be too bad."

Tomas just looked to the window, where the sun was sinking. There seemed to be more people around the house now, and they started humming as the sun touched the horizon.

"Where is Señor Torrez?" Otis said. "He has had plenty of time."

Suddenly Millie had a horrifying thought. *What was Señor Torrez doing in the street of the witches? There is only one person he could do business for there — Wanunu! Even the hotel where we stayed in Arica had statues to honor Pachamama. Señor Torrez is not coming with Charles's bag, and he did not tell Don Rael where we are. I am sure of it. He is a worshiper of Pachamama himself!*

Tomas closed the shutters on the window now, latching it as if to keep out the night, but Millie could still see the sun through cracks in the wood. It sank quickly now, like a ball of fire disappearing into the mountain.

Thump! Millie turned to see Tupac on the floor, his back arched and his limbs shaking. Charles was at his side before Millie reached him. The little boy's eyes were rolled back in his head.

"Seizure!" Charles said. "Let's get him onto his bed." He lifted the small body in his arms and put it on the mat. "I don't understand this," he said. "He was fine a moment ago. Now he is burning up." Millie put her hand against the boy's head. It was blazing hot.

"We have to reduce the fever," Charles said. "That's what's causing the seizure."

There was a sound of whispered mourning outside of the house, a movement, and the candles Tomas was lighting flickered. The darkness seemed to press in from the corners of the room, pushing against the candlelight.

"Charles," Millie said, "it's time to stand."

Charles stopped in mid-step. He seemed to know instantly what she meant. "Jesus, we ask You to protect the life of this child!" he prayed. Suddenly, Tupac was shaking so violently his teeth rattled. Tomas pulled the covers over him, looking to Charles and Millie with pleading in his eyes. "In the name of Jesus, you will not take his life!" Charles declared, and Tupac moaned.

"Let me hold him," Millie said. She took the small body in her arms, and her heart ached to feel him shaking with cold chills while at the same time he was hot with fever. Millie sat in the rocking chair with Tupac against her shoulder. She could still feel the darkness all around like a dark tornado, probing the walls of the building like whispers of fear, but she heard something else as well.

Millie knew that still, quiet voice. She had heard it before in sickrooms and on her quiet walks. "Will you hand me my Bible, Otis?" she asked. She held the boy against her shoulder with one hand, and with the other she opened her Bible to Psalm 91 and began to read.

"He who dwells in the shelter of the Most High will rest in the shadow of the Almighty. I will say of the Lord, 'He is my refuge and my fortress, my God, in whom I trust.' Surely he will save you from the fowler's snare and from the deadly pestilence. He will cover you with his feathers, and under his wings you will find refuge; his faithfulness will be your shield and rampart. You will not fear the terror of night, nor the arrow that flies by day, nor the pestilence that stalks in the darkness, nor the plague that destroys at midday."

She made the words a prayer, crying out to God for the little life that rested in her arms, and she could sense the darkness drawing back.

"A thousand may fall at your side, ten thousand at your right hand, but it will not come near you." Millie felt the shivers leave the small body, and Tupac relaxed against her. Millie looked up for the first time, and saw Charles and Otis standing over her, their eyes closed in prayer.

Tupac shuddered when she stopped reading, and Millie went back to the page. "You will only observe with your eyes and see the punishment of the wicked. If you make the Most High your dwelling—even the Lord, who is my refuge—then no harm will befall you, no disaster will come near your tent."

The psalm was a promise for this small boy, Millie was sure of it. The certainty of it raised goose bumps along her arms and sent chills down her spine, but still she read. "For he will command his angels concerning you to guard you in all your ways; they will lift you up in their hands, so that you will not strike your foot against a stone…. 'Because he loves me,' says the Lord, 'I will rescue him; I will protect him, for he acknowledges my name.' "

Millie felt as if she were sitting in a puddle of light, and the darkness swirling around her was not allowed in.

" 'He will call upon me, and I will answer him; I will be with him in trouble, I will deliver him and honor him. With long life will I satisfy him and show him my salvation.' "

There were tears on her cheeks when she finished the psalm, but still the little one on her shoulder did not stir. Charles took the Bible from her, and Tomas held his arms out for his brother.

And so they passed the night in prayer and Bible reading, while the destroyer, like a lion, was prowling just outside the circle of light, unable to come in. They took turns reading psalms of praise and warfare, promises of God, and all the while Tomas held Tupac close to his heart.

At last the sun came up, and the grey dawn sky outside the window turned blue. Tomas lifted his head. "Tupac," he whispered. "Tupac!"

The little boy opened his eyes and smiled up at his brother. Tomas shouted and held him up at arm's length, then spun him around. Then Tomas spun Charles, Otis, and Millie around as well, jumping from one to another and shouting with joy.

He gave his brother curds and parched grain to eat, and watched every bite disappear before he offered the same to his guests. When they had eaten, Tomas wrapped his brother in a blanket, lifted him onto his shoulders, picked up his shovel, and opened the door.

Millie's Reluctant Sacrifice

"Where is he going?" Millie asked.

"I believe he is going to dig a foundation," Charles said. The watchers were still outside the house, and they gasped when Tupac waved to them. Slowly the men and women fell into line behind them, following Tomas up the hill.

He set Tupac on the dirt with a blanket wrapped around him, and began to dig. One by one, the men of the village joined them.

Señor Torrez rode up and sat silently, his face unreadable.

Wanunu came last, hobbling as if she had injured herself in the night. She pointed to Millie and began to speak.

"What is she saying, señor?" Millie asked. But he was silent.

"Tell us!" Otis commanded.

"She says that you have not won the victory you think," he said evenly. "She let the child live because Pachamama wants another." To Millie's shock, a wicked smile slithered across his face—the first smile she had seen from him since they met. "But because you have defied her," he continued, pointing at Millie, "the goddess will take from you what you love best—she will take your husband's life!"

Millie finds herself embroiled in spiritual warfare for a Bolivian town. When her faith is tested, will Millie stand?

MILLIE'S FIERY TRIAL

Book Eight
of the
*A Life of Faith:
Millie Keith* Series

Published by Mission City Press
Committed to helping today's girls develop a LIFE of faith!

For more information about
A Life of Faith™ books, dolls, and companion products,
write to Mission City Press, Inc.,
P.O. Box 681913, Franklin, TN 37068-1913

Collect all of our Millie products!

Collect our other
A *Life of Faith* Products!

A *Life of Faith: Elsie Dinsmore*

— ABOUT THE AUTHOR —

$\mathcal{M}$artha Finley was born on April 26, 1828, in Chillicothe, Ohio. Her mother died when Martha was quite young, and Dr. James Finley, her father, soon remarried. Martha's stepmother, Mary Finley, was a kind and caring woman who always nurtured Martha's desire to learn and supported her ambition to become a writer.

Dr. Finley was a physician and a devout Christian gentleman. He moved his family to South Bend, Indiana, in the mid-1830s in hopes of a brighter future for his family on the expanding western frontier. Growing up on the frontier as one of eight brothers and sisters surely provided the setting and likely many of the characters for Miss Finley's *Mildred Keith* novels. Considered by many to be partly autobiographical, the books present a fascinating and devoted Christian heroine in the fictional character known as Millie Keith. One can only speculate exactly how much of Martha may have been Millie and vice versa. But regardless, these books nicely complement Miss Finley's bestselling *Elsie Dinsmore* series, which was launched in 1868 and sold millions of copies. The stories of Millie Keith, Elsie's second cousin, were released eight years after the *Elsie* books as a follow-up to that series.

Martha Finley never married and never had children of her own, but she was a remarkable woman who lived a quiet life of creativity and Christian charity. She died at age 81, having written many novels, stories, and books for children and adults. Her life on earth ended in 1909, but her legacy lives on in the wonderful stories of Millie and Elsie.

Check out
www.alifeoffaith.com

- Get news about Millie and her cousin Elsie
- Find out more about the 19th century world they live in
- Learn to live a life of faith like they do
- Learn how they overcome the difficulties we all face in life
- Find out about Millie and Elsie products
- Join our girls' club

A Life of Faith Books
"It's Like Having a Best Friend From Another Time"

Beloved Literary Characters *Come to Life!*

*Y*our favorite heroines, Elsie Dinsmore and Millie Keith, are now available as lovely designer dolls from Mission City Press.

*M*ade of soft-molded vinyl, these beautiful, fully-jointed 18¾" dolls come dressed in historically-accurate clothing and accessories. They wonderfully reflect the Biblical virtues that readers have come to know and love about Elsie and Millie.

For more information, visit www.alifeoffaith.com or check with your local Christian retailer.

A Life of Faith Products from Mission City Press

"It's Like Having a Best Friend From Another Time"